FINDING LIGHT

ANTHONY UNGER and AMBER UNGER

Finding Light

ISBN 978-1-09839-529-2
eBook ISBN 978-1-09839-530-8

TABLE OF CONTENTS

*-(Previously written) *The Purple Dot* was published in 2018, in a school magazine.

FOREWORD

'Finding Light' is an unconnected sequel to Morweena Christian School (MCS, which happens to be in the small village of Morweena, North-West of Arborg, Manitoba) 2012's Flower Garden, which is an anthology written by a class of high-schoolers. *'Finding Light,'* however, sets a new theme in which all twelve stories share a theme that differs in each story, but still keeps the idea of being able to find a solution in each of our problems. Each story brings a new idea but the overall beginning, middle, and end, come together to create a trilogy. The *Child of the Cube* trilogy is a psychological idea that horrified the author to even make it a part of this book. And even though it sounds like this anthology is going to be dark, don't worry, it still finds light.

—Anthony Unger

P.S: I admit that the title had another reason to be what it is. I subconsciously picked it when I felt most hopeless in January 2020. This book was one of the ways I found light, found hope. And I say this because I struggle with completing books. This is an example that I, and all authors in the world, can finish the art that they start. Back to the title: it reminds me of my mortality and the main trilogy represents the dark, hopeless things we experience in our lives. By the time you reach the end of each story hope is somehow found in multiple different ways. *Finding Light* can mean multiple different things and this book is only a small sliver of the iceberg. In a way, *Finding Light* is like searching for trust in a world where it's hard to find trust. It's when it feels like there's no light in the dark when really there's just as much light as darkness. It's a relief, a gift, an answer and solution, or a way around an obstacle.

Acknowledgements: Thank you to the beta-readers, who helped this anthology come to be. You know who you are if you've read one of these stories before publication. And thanks to our cover designer for giving the anthology an image.

000002IIII000002IIIII 000002IIIII200000000IIIIIIIII000002IIII0000000

THE CHILD OF THE CUBE
1

It all began with the taste of breakfast on my buds. The walls had provided a mixture of two pancakes, bacon, and an infamous omelet with a thin slathering of maple syrup. Now, this is sustenance to me, even possibly better than supper. Which is unmentionable due to its feasting size. All this food and drink was provided by a thin tube hanging from a circular pod. Now that it had finished filling my empty stomach after waking from rest, it receded from the corners of my sight. With a sliding bang, its nonexistence was confirmed. It was no longer a part of this room. This was an ordinary room, to me at least. But it was also a horror and oddity. A place of four sides, all a different shade. Grey, White, Black, and whatever was in between. “What’s another shade?” I asked the grey wall before me. It, she…, didn’t answer. Thinking up a word for the wall behind me, I took what Grey had once said in account. She had had a name for it. A name I found was perfect because I was at a loss at what to describe its emptiness. Grey had said that it was not Black, Grey, or White. Instead, it was apparently more of a brighter white, a brighter grey, and a brighter black put together to something she called bright. And so that’s what was behind me, a bright wall. In front of me was Grey, to my right was White, my left, Black, and behind me, was Bright. I had a name to match each part of my surroundings. My surroundings, a box. A cube that has a hold on my very being, and it keeps me where I am. I can’t see behind me, only presume from what I hear. And this is where I fall on a new problem. The ceiling and floor have no name. They are just more sides in a cube. One above, one below. If you were to change the physics of this cube, up would be down, ceiling would be floor. So therefore the wall above is wall number five, whilst the floor is number six. The life I know has six walls, the open world I theorize, does too. The only way I can be sure of this theory being true is by finding a way out. But for now, the only life I know is the cube. I have never stepped foot into the open world, or at least I don’t think so. All I know is that I was born here seventy years ago. And the only reason I know about the open world is through the walls. They show me what happens in the open world. To be precise, only the first four walls can speak to me. Or at least those are the only voices I hear aside from my own. They have told me stories that frighten me. Stories of monsters and their terrible acts. But after being here for as long as I remember, I wonder if there is any possibility of it being better than the cube. This place is maddening with its lack of freedom. Nothing here truly makes sense and I have a feeling it shouldn't exist. There is more to these brief moments of the cube as I fall to darkness after every moment. So, I have come to a decision; I must escape to the open world. Maybe I belong there, not here where I'm the only one of my kind. Once there, I will also see everything that the walls have talked about. To really know if what they say is true. The words they use after all are hard to trust, I've been around them for far too long. I attempt to look past the line of vision, not being able to move my head. All I can see and ever will be able to see is a colour like no other. It's different from all the rest, worth no words I can muster. Except maybe the two silent ones. An indistinguishable voice from one of the walls reminded me that my nap had arrived. I feel my very essence becoming a dark cloud. The air, of what there is of it, smelled metallic and clung to the skin. It made my nostrils burn. I have felt, I have seen, all of this before. And like all of those other times I have experienced this, my mind goes blank. Then, my vision grows nil.

2

The nap is finished. And I'm back to standing in the very center of my prison. I'm like a statue that can't move. Although statues in general are stone beings that don't make movement a habit. This is one of the many things White has told me. As for standing, the walls state that I've been on this same spot for as long as I've lived. I know I have, but I don't want to believe it. I do believe that I've been here for some time, kept against my will, persuaded that I belong here. But how can I belong when I just stand here without much activity? All I've ever done is watch the open world through the walls open mouths. The only way I can keep mentality is by thinking and this alone drives me mad. I'm starting to fall apart after so long, I must escape! I must see the world that is dreaded by my parents. And from this world I see the past, and only the past. The wars that run like a plague, and the immorality that never ends. This is what I see as I gaze into what Grey's showing me. Her mouth changes images as my daily spill begins. Horrific things make it into my mind and

I attempt to look away. But I can't; I just can't. And if I could, the spill, a load of history and information, would still pull me in with its claws. I'm not in control of myself. My family, the six sides of the cube, are my puppeteers. Bright says he's my father and both White, and Black, say they're my brother and sister. Finally, the grey wall in front of me states that she's my mother. And thinking of my parents, I have never seen my father. I've only heard mention of his shade and wrath from my mother, and siblings. They say once I see him, I'll meet death. But I don't know this death they speak of. So every time they mention him, or it, I ask about death. They say no more. Is he a good soul, or is he like my father? This is something I simply don't know. Something I do know is that I must escape this prison to save my sanity. That is, if sanity's even a good thing. How do I know this is real? How do I know this isn't a dream? How do I know I'm not insane? I've got it; I am insane. How else do I explain this maddening place that never ends? How else do I explain the feeling of not being who I am? My thoughts suddenly grow silent, and the spill ends. A voice breaks the glass of this stillness. It's the grey wall. Mother speaks.

"What is this useless babble you think, Child?"

"I'm not thinking, Mother. I swear I'm not."

"What!" she exclaims with an expression on her ridged appearance. All you can see is a pair of black, thin eyebrows and a protruding nose with the outline of a mouth.

"I'm not talking," I lie to the grey wall.

"But you are. You're talking with invisible words I can still hear."

I ponder over it and then answer in shame, "I confess; I lied to you about thinking. It's impossible, Mother. I can't live without thought. It would mean my mind was dormant. Therefore, without a mind, I can't exist as a logical being," I stifle a nervous laugh.

"You lie, Child. Thought is illogical. I only wish you would remember that you can by no means think. And you shall absolutely not talk if not spoken to. You have done wrong once again, and I have run out of patience for your kind. We as the cube tried to make you perfect like us. I tried to train a human. But now I realize that that was a useless effort," she scoffed with a belief that the walls were superior.

"What I have done is part of human beings. I haven't made a mistake, and it's true, we're imperfect. I realized it later than I should've. You lied to me; you're not my mother. The open world is where I belong. Not here. Not in the cube. Not in this madness."

"Humph! Do not remember what I said before! This is the last time you'll ever commit another fault. First, you tried to see your father, and now you defy what I say. Goodbye, child of the cube! This is the end. It's time for you to meet your real father!"

"I'm sorry, Mother. Please, I don't want to. I won't turn back; I won't think. Please, I don't want to see father; I don't want to meet death."

It's too late. My body is figuratively thawing. I'm moving and I can't stop it. I can't stop this life that's flowing through me. A part of me is terrified of seeing what's out of my vision, but another part is relieved. This might be a promise of freedom. My arms are now moving. I'm moving them. I'm pretending to resist… to fool mother. I mustn't see the unseen; I'll die. But this means escape; it must. I'll be able to see the open world. I'm lowering my arms now. This is it; I've turned all the way around. I'm free.

"Stop bickering, Human. You are no longer my child; I banish thee!" Father's looking at me with anger. He is bright; they were telling the truth. The wall's brighter than all light inside the cube. It then turned to an inward opening leading into an abyss. This is a confrontation of darkness. And I have faith that is starting to grow dimmer. I'm doubting the freedom that I've been promised. It's more of a hope for this death to be the end of this insanity. Preferably it's a glance of the open world. A small glance, at least. All thought vanishes in an instant. I'm swallowed up by the dark abyss, and the cube is turned into nothingness, once again.

3

A new sensation breaks the dark ether as I'm taken away and to a familiar corridor. A familiarity I can't place for the life of me. With an abrupt pull I'm being led down a walkway reminding me of prison. A punishing sector that I had only seen from Grey's screen. I was being led by the strings that lead to the one puppeteering my advancement down the corridor. There's nothing I can do to halt the movement I make. I am not in control. I'm not who I am. Several flashes of colour lash out at me as lights flicker to black. The strings belonging to the puppeteer then snap, leaving my feet to do the running. Then all of a sudden, arms shoot out from either side of the corridor, attempting to drag me closer to them. I'm not safe and most of all, I'm scared. Scared of the dark. Scared of the walls. This can't be freedom. For it's worse than the cube. I was wrong; death wasn't someone to mess with. This was death, and all I can do is run. I don't even know what freedom is anymore. I just want to get out of this nightmare. Perhaps this is how insanity feels like. Perhaps this is really just sanity in disguise. Is this sanity, or insanity? This question lingers in my mind as walls close in, making it hard for me to breathe. I trip over something unknown in the darkness and fall to the mysterious ground. I must get out of here; this can't be freedom. For if I stay any longer, I will be crushed by the stone sides of the corridor as they shift towards me. A light emanates at the end of the corridor. And without hesitation, I push myself away from where I'm hunched on the ground. I'm running again and this time, I have somewhere to run to. This time, nothing is stopping me and I take the chance to escape by reaching the doorway of brightness. The light engulfs its enemy and I'm left in despair. I am surrounded by walls. Walls that are different but very much the same as the last. They have similar colours, but this time they've been variated. The wall on my right is Black, left is a tint of Dark-Silver, and the wall directly in front is Grey. Grey has never changed. Mother is still there. And that stillness that was once in my bones is again there. I can't move my body. I'm frozen. Therefore, I can't see my new father. I turn my head as much as I can, moving my eyes to glimpse at the tip of a ceiling and the bottom. And the bottom.... Wait, no! The bottom wall is nothing and has no face. That's why they were the silent ones; they weren't walls. There is nothing supporting my feet. I'm going to fall into what I no longer believe is freedom. Except, I'm not falling; I'm still in the cube. I can't see what's happening but I can sense a change. The room is getting smaller as I think these thoughts. And with a burst of strength, I can move. I'm turning around and no one is controlling me. My eyes fill up with tears. This is my nightmare. This is my never-ending nightmare. But this time, everything's wrong. Father's gone from behind me. Which means that there's only one last place where he could've gone. He's the wall that should've been underneath me. I glance down, seeing the entirety of the floor. I'm not going to fall. With an inkling of hope, I fall. Time doesn't give me the chance to cry out as I leave my prison in a downward flight.

4

A green surface rushes up to meet my covered feet. Which subsequently led to my body rolling to protect them from breaking. But the rolling never stops. I keep descending at an angle, down a lush, green hill. The rolling then slows down and stops, leaving me breathless. Picking myself up with difficulty, I whisper quietly to myself, "Freedom, at last." Having seen relatively nothing of this land I survey, the green hill dipped down into a valley. All around the valley, mountains tipped with snow stood like guardians silently watching. Silently, like the ceiling and the floor. I dread the memories of the cube. Threading down the valley's summit, on the flattest section of ground, is a large, white dome. Spires reach to the sky like fingers. And small, black dots fly around, what I presume is a city. Something tells me that this is not from my time. Nonetheless, all of this feels too real not to be. And therefore, it can't be a nightmare. I've escaped the cube. I look to where I fell, but there's nothing indicating the cube was ever there. It was like my nightmare never existed. It's gone now; that's all that's important right now. I carefully amble down the rest of the hill until the grass ends and dirt replaces it. Then, a dozen footsteps later I realize I can't reach the city. It keeps on moving every time I get closer. It's stepping back while I step forward. I should've figured it out sooner. This is too good to be true. Freedom was never at my fingertips. Instead, I'm still in my nightmare. I can see the walls now. A ghostly image of them is getting more concrete over the scenery I'm a part of. They rise behind the mountains and higher before they meet together to form four corners in the sky. Amidst the corners, a purple hue pigments the heavens in one blink. I'm still inside the cube. This strange world disappears and the shaded box is back. My sanity still stays broken and escape is only an impossible dream now. I fall to my knees, begging for it anyway. With my hands intertwined, I plead for freedom. Whatever this is I call life, it's not what I want. There is more. The grey wall speaks. The city in the valley brought the truth out. How, I don't know, but it's somehow connected to who I am. My determination to escape has also been rebooted. I must escape sooner than ever if I want my mind to survive. I have hope I'll escape the cube. I must have freedom.

"What? This isn't possible! You should be gone by now! Gone from our presence! I have tried to teach you, pet! Don't come back! Don't try to avoid your fate!"

I'm speechless as I watch the grey wall contort in a protruding grimace. Her words are replaced by serenity, which are taken by a sharp sound that pierces my ears. Hands immediately shoot out to protect them but the sound soon morphs into laughter. The walls are calling me names now that churn up the despair. Names like circle face, yellow-head, and the worst of all, the insane loafer. I don't have the slightest idea what the latter means, but I don't like the sound of it. I'm starting to break again and so I scream at them. But they just retort back.

"But you are. You are. You're an ugly loafer cause all you do is stand there, doing nothing. Nothing at all. Nothing at all. Mother tried to train you, make you logical. Except, we all know now that you're not worth it. Not worth it at all."

The walls taunt me as I sit there on my knees, trying to ignore what they say. They try their hardest to keep me from freedom. Like tricksters, which is what they are. But that doesn't stop me as I'm overcome with power to fight back. It's like someone beside the walls is watching. I don't know who, but they're also not the mountains.

"I'm not going to let you bombard me with lies. None of this is my fault. And that name doesn't bother me 'cause I would if I could. I would move if I could. I'm not insane. I'm not. You are the ones that...," I'm still on my knees but now consciousness is starting to leave. When will the ending of a moment, and the beginning of another, stop? I can feel myself topple over in a mess. But no matter how much I try, I'll never be rid of the cube. I'll never have freedom.

5

I wake up with arms that I cannot move. They're indisposed. And this world I was trapped in, I'm not sure if it ever existed or not. It is merely a broken part of my broken mind. Henceforth, I shall treat it as an apparition of the mind. It was a fake reality. I am now in what I can perceive as real. However, just like the nightmare, I am constrained. The more I struggle, the noisier the bell clangs at the side of the bed. This sends the dark notion that I'm still in a prison, through my very mind. I sit up and it's not long before the ringing achieves its purpose. The room I'm in is brightly-lit until it darkens with tall, faceless forms. My vision is being crowded and it hurts my eyes to keep them open. It's another nightmare. Except this time, I don't think it's fake. Struggling to tear off the confinement, I'm pushed back onto the bed. My arms are somehow a part of what imprison me. And there's a name for it on the tip of my tongue. It's a straitjacket. One of the figures disappears into an area beyond what I can see. Then it comes back, holding a thin object between a few fingers.

"Relax, Arthur, everything will be alright. I'm just going to make those nightmares go away. And this is what's going to do it. It'll make you go sleepy-sleep. There's no freedom; there never was," the ominous and calm voice tries to reassure me. Of course, I doubt this and keep on fighting back. It repeats over and over, never stopping. So my real name is Arthur. And the question I asked before in the cube, sanity or insanity, I think I know the answer. I'm trapped in my own reality. The thing is: it's worse than the nightmare I tried to run from. It's the reality where my answer isn't what I want it to be. This reality, I'm trying to run from it. And as the thin object comes closer and closer, I have time to blurt out my last sentence. Before I feel the small pain of breaking skin I utter one four-word line. Repeatedly spoken in a faltering breath. Child of the cube, child of the cube. And when the time was still available, I complimented the sentence. I am, the child of the cube.

IIIIIIII000002IIIIIIII:

TALL

It was 1965, but things weren't how they were supposed to be. One small detail had been changed by a power-hungry alien race. For the longest time, the alien race had been unnamed. But when the humans realized something was different from what they perceived as normal, they all thought the same thought. The aliens, being telepathic, understood it was time to reveal themselves. When their name was revealed to the humans, it was so long that everyone agreed on a shorter name that was easier to remember. They were called the Fallokratists, which was later shortened to the 'Falls'. These Falls were experimenting and were once banished from their home planet, Farlos, for experimenting with their own kind. At least, that's what they had said when they announced that the normality change was because of them. They had announced this as a transmission to everyone, sparking more fear than ever. The humans, no matter who they were or where they were, looked up as a telepathic link was made and a face of strange conformities looked down at them. "Good day, earthlings! We are an alien race from the planet Farlos! Call us the Fallokratists. You have been administered a shot of our height-growth formula and guess what, we won't reverse its effects. You will stay like this to become our lab rats and we will study you."

"It's an invasion!" someone in Puerto Rico cried in fright as others in Russia, America, Canada and so forth did as well.

"Invade your planet! We want no planet, especially a ruined and rat-infested place like it. No, we only want the results of our experiment," the Fallokratist spokeperson grimaced and then chuckled in the minds of many. The statement turned into a speech that went on for another two minutes. Apparently ever since the experiments on Farlos, their curious nature had moved to a new type of life and a new subject of interest had been formed, the earthlings. And not too long, at 8.00 am eastern time, a press of a button aboard the Falls' star-ship caused a group of radioactive waves to wash over the earth in a green coat. Of course, for some people it happened overnight, and the others, in the day. This subject of interest was a question on what would happen if a human attribute was changed. Would the entire population start decreasing overtime or would it fall quickly and in a short time? This change was directed towards being born. Not just that, a law of physics and biology was being broken. Everyone alive started to shrink according to their age while every baby that was born was starting to grow abnormally tall. Everybody at the age of fifty and over shrunk to about four feet, while the youngest of the humans started growing in height. The foreign race had changed the method a human grew. Twenty-eight-year-old Vanessa Twinning had a son today. He had been born healthy and normal but when the nurses went to check up on him, they knew something wasn't right. The small, transparent box that had held the newborn was now in pieces. Not just that; instead of being small, he was exactly seven feet and six inches in height. The wheeled table had been broken as well and now the baby lay on the ground in a very unhappy mood. In the doorway to the room, the two nurses gaped with open mouths as the three newborns in the baby room cried in their new state. It would be a very long shift for the two and a long explanation would be needed. An explanation that would leave everyone baffled, especially Vanessa and her husband. Their lives had just taken a turn due to the unexpected incident and the biological significance it held. And it was very true that everything should have been fine, but it hadn't been. Now, mothers were feeling the same way all over the globe. They blamed themselves for their children's deformities and the only way it could be reversed was through the Falls. This, in turn, could only be achieved by making an agreement with them or using military force. Now, who could make an agreement with them but the people who called themselves leaders of the world? The most powerful people of the world held a meeting and that proved one thing. The government were cowards regarding extra-terrestrial matters. That meant only half of them wanted to communicate with the aliens while the rest formed a rebelling alliance that believed in force. The leader of the negotiation side with its small numbers, was the director of NASA, Alvin Coratio. Now, he had made a call to an old friend who owed him. Coratio had once aided him to stop the assassination of the president. The question was now which side would enact their solution first—the rebels with violence on their minds or the negotiators with their peaceful tactics. One thing was for sure; the negotiators' operative was here. John Vauge, a navy seal who was now confidently striding into NASA's luxurious lobby, was the operative. The lobby had a lotta red, a chandelier, and had a similar resemblance to a hotel lobby. Vauge had sandy-brown hair, a face that couldn't stay cold, and was tanned with a deep brown. He also had the most sixty-ish wear you'd ever see. His eyes were covered by a pair of red-tinted shades that were later placed in a shirt pocket, and he wore colourful attire that Joseph with his coat would be proud of. Joseph, the one who had been betrayed by his brothers long ago. The rest of his attire included a silver necklace promoting peace and a pair of camouflage khakis that went well with his dull boots. If you ever thought this man was violent, you would be very wrong. John Vauge was one of the nicest people you would ever meet. He was a people person and his sister, Tracie, doubted very much that could ever be changed. The noisy stepping, thanks to his heavy footwear, took him to the counter. His arrival at the counter was aided by another's presence. There, sitting at a velvet office chair, facing away from him, was a brunette John thought to be in her twenties. Her fingers danced across a typewriter with the keys a'clacking. He rang the little golden bell that sat by itself on the pinewood countertop. Of course, with no luck at diverting her attention.

"Well, I guess I'm going to wait here for three years and by then these arrogant Falls will have changed our hair as well. My full head of hair will be replaced by some alien equivalent. Maybe a high fluff of tentacles. And must I mention that I'm thirty-nine and I'm definitely ten inches shorter than I was yesterday. Heck, I actually don't care about what happens today as long as the Falls literally fall from their notion of superiority; I repeat, the Falls have fallen, the Falls have fallen." Vauge opened his eyes from the one second close to see a disgruntled secretary that soon changed to a faintly smiling secretary.

"Hmm, funny. I should add that to my story," the secretary went back to typing and the retired navy seal was left waiting. The only upside to this was that she was wearing a name tag on her rose-coloured cardigan.

"Which way to Coratio's office?"

Nothing. She ignored him as if no one was even there. He tried again. "I could get you fired, but instead, I'm going to buy your story, Jessica."

She automatically turned to face him with a look of optimism. "Really, you're going to buy it? You don't even know what it's about."

His face transitioned from a grinning nature to a stern look that led to an observant reply. "It's about the Falls, and here you go," he passed the bill across the counter with his grin back in its rightful place. "Oh, and by the way, it's called 'Tall.'"

She retorted with a, "What do you mean? I haven't named it yet," as she graciously took the money.

And of course Vauge answered back, "exactly." Now Jessica was both taken aback and excited that someone actually wanted to read her piece of writing. The exchange of money had broken her optimism that no one alive cared about the content that she wrote. She wanted this to be a discussion and for him to read it. But now wasn't the time and she could see that he was in a hurry so she directed him to the first door on floor three. "Thank you," he softly spoke. Vauge's feet then took him to the silver wall that served as a two-part door to the elevator, not too far away from the counter. A press of a button located to the left of the wall, caused both sides of the elevator door to shutter. Then a few seconds later, it opened to release a sight of cushioned walls in more dark-red. He quickly became a part of the elevator with it's velveteen-cushioned walls, dark-coloured ceiling and silver-grated floor. And on the other side of the two-buttoned panel was another one, this time inside the movable box. With a swift movement from his right hand, he pushed a circlet with the number three designed neatly on it. The rest of the dull circlets were untouched, leaving a sunken brother behind. Then the contraption burst into action, giving him the impression his first elevator would be rather eventful. It wasn't and instead he stood in silence until life halted for the motion that moved the small space. The double doors opened and he was let out into a hallway of doors. With it a haze of cigarette smoke filled his nostrils. The hallway also had a fair share of people tending to their day and in a place like this; the future was now. John navigated through the constant stream of bodies and soon found himself at a glass-paneled door. A coppery name-plate on the door read, 'Director Alvin Coratio.' The American knocked on the door and a deep voice boomed approval.[1]The doors quickly set aside in a matter of seconds and indeed closed, once again. Vauge was left in a windowed room where a gray fan spun at a casual speed. At the side of the farthest window of the room was a cherry wood desk holding a plump, short man behind it. The desk was surprisingly neat and organized alongside an ashtray where he stored his used-up cigarette butts. However, today wasn't a good day to smoke, but once this was all over, he wouldn't deny the guilty pleasure. The director was an old fifty, so he would now be shorter than the last time Vauge had met him. Coratio had a blooming scalp of inky black and an elegant nose that fit well with his face.

"John Vauge, they say you're done with the seals. They also say you're done helping your country out. But personally, I don't think you are. I mean, you did come when I called you from your

---

1 *Just a side note: I think Director Alvin Coratio would be played well by the infamous Patrick Warburton in a film adaptation. That won't happen though, and that is fine.

cottage by the sea," Coratio opened a drawer in the desk. This was followed by him pulling a bottle of his sharpest, most expensive wine from it.

"You know, Coratio, I would like to be done with it all. However, it pulls me in as soon as I'm out. It's the sinking sands of my full, chaotic life. Though I think there are times when I value them for what they are. They bring me reasons to live, help me find purpose in it all," Coratio pulled a pair of shot glasses and a cork-screw from the drawer. After that, he pulled the cork loose and then poured half a glass for him and his operative.

A loud laugh echoed from the director's throat. "Come, sit down; I believe we both know what's at stake here. Here's some wine; it's the best I've got," a serious tone leaked into the plump man's jovial nature. As he was smiling, Vauge took the shot glass and sat down on one of two very comfy-looking chairs. Coratio took no hesitation as he swished the liquid down and then started pouring another.

"I do. But sometimes, I doubt if you even know half of the time what it is," a grin emerged on his lips.

"Well it's true. I don't half of the time. Except, this time we know very well what's at stake. An old normal is about to turn to a new normal if we don't act, soon," he replied with sincerity. He then offered John another drink as he finished his as well. But not being an alcoholic in any particular way, he refused and put the glass down on the desk.

"The normality of us humans," a whisper from John's tongue made the words quiet and gave it certain urgency.

"Exactly, John," Coratio wagged a forefinger at his old friend.

"I don't want to do it."

"Just wait, John. You'll want to hear the rest. 'Cause that there what you said, that's how I know you'll never stop doing what you can for the human race. You care too much about life and now Earth needs someone who cares, and someone with a persuasive tongue. Earth needs someone to negotiate with the Falls. Make them see eye to eye on what we think of their messing around."

"What of the rebels?" He let down his face, not really wanting to be there for anything that would put him in one of Coratio's situations. "You know what happens when two sides fight to succeed in their aims. It creates a war, director, a war," Vauge said as he crossed his arms. The idea of a war starting due to this experiment was something not worth thinking about, but he did it anyway. "War; I've learnt to live with. But I'm telling you; whatever you want me to do, I'm not doing it. I'm retired from everything, not just the seals. I'm retired from saving the world."

"I know. It's going to be chaos, but I also know you're good with getting rid of chaos. And I've gotta say we have to do something quick. They're planning to launch a hybrid missile that at impact with the Fall ship will release a serum called the Jeong-gyuseong, or the Jeong serum for short," Coratio said.

"They got it from the Koreans?"

"It seems so. But how, no one knows. That information, they say, is closed to everyone but their side of the argument. All we know is that Jeong-gyuseong means, 'normality.'"

"I'm presuming you're not going to pursue anything about how they got the serum?" Vauge asked.

"You're right in presuming so, Vauge. We'll just stick with the negotiation method. The reason for that...," he took the words from Vauge before he had a chance to use them, "...is that the rebels have stated that they'll give us the first move. And we don't want to do anything that might change their minds. Their cure might not be needed if our peaceful tactics work on those blasted aliens!" Director Coratio was interrupted just as he knotted his fists together.

"They're not blasted; they're green, director," Vauge joked with a mild grin.

Coratio sarcastically returned with, "Ha ha! Anyway, back to what I was saying. If the negotiations on our end don't work by ten tonight, then the Jeong serum is activated. It then makes its way down until it passes through earth's protective shield. From there on, it causes a chemical reaction that creates moisture in the air, which then turns to rain," he put both palms flat on the cherry wood desk.

"Let me guess; rain plus serum equals a happy ending," the retired navy seal uncrossed his arms then set them on the chair's arms. Taking off his right hand from its rest, he held his chin.

"Something like that, yeah. I, however, don't buy it. It all sounds like hogwash. But that doesn't mean it won't have consequences. Instead, it'll mean that life is over as we know it. Anyway, I've talked to the board of directors here at NASA. They're after all the ones who agreed with my method, and they gave an all go that action must be taken. We humans must retake our dignity, put things back to mankind's original setting.

That means that we must act now, pronto! What do you say? You're in?".

"What do I say? You should've called me sooner, Director."

"I know. I know. Trust me when I say I tried. You were on vacation."

"I was joking. And yes, I was supposed to be, but I found something disturbing in the Pacific Ocean."

"Pray tell, Vauge," the director replied.

"That's classified, director," Vauge loosened up. "But I will say one thing. A ship of dolls."

The director sensed he didn't want to talk about it and went with his tempting offer. "What do you say, Vauge? Don't give me no baloney. What do you say? Are you in?"

"Wait, Coratio. If I say yes, what if while I'm negotiating with the Falls, something goes wrong? What if I say something that agitates them, and they release more of their experimental minds on us?"

"Don't worry, Vauge, everything's going to be fine. For the most part. And remember, if you say no, you will never have to come back again. When I call and message you to come and help the world out, it won't be you; it will be a replacement. Oh and by the time that happens, we'll be short to the point of microscopic. 'Cause as you can guess, no one likes doing anything for poor Coratio," saying so, Alvin scrunched up his eyes and rolled his fists under them.

"You have a replacement for me?"

"We won't talk about that. Now, how about you make up your mind?"

[2]-Vauge says yes: stay on page

Vauge says no: turn to page 35

After a minute of thought, the retired navy seal answered, though with a slight grumble. "You make it sound rather thrilling to be the first to talk to an alien. And being a true born Vauge, I gotta say yes," he stood up, followed by Coratio.

---

2 Originally, this story was never going to be a decision making-based matter but I had an idea to spice it up a bit by creating two endings. So in the end it became my very first double-ending short.)

"Good; I've already arranged everything, so follow me."

Just like that, the two exited the small office before making their way through the hazy corridor. The corridor ended and all that was left was another translucent door and name plate—the meeting and operations room. It was opened by Coratio's hand to shower the two pairs of eyes with a dim-lit room. Inside was a sharply rounded table that was centered and fit with a communications setup. Three men sat around the table and John presumed they were there to ensure that everything went as planned. On each of their heads was a pair of headphones that were connected by black cords to an outlet on the setup. This would relay the Falls' transmission directly to this room. And in return, it would pick up Vauge's transmission, and equally broadcast it to the Falls.

Coratio directed John's attention to each of the three men's faces. Then he said, "This here is Alistair. He's recording the broadcast for our records. That's Martin; he's the engineer that made the state of the art communicator. And lastly, the guy in the tie, smoking the cig, is Oscar White. He paid to get a front row seat and that's what he got."

"You mean the millionaire Oscar White?" Vauge chuckled.

"The one and only," the man on the farthest right known as Oscar, handed a sheaf of paper to Coratio. "And guess what? We had him write us up a pretty darn good script," the stapled bundle of paper went into the operative's hands with a final pass. The director then glimpsed the script over with a reassurance that everything would go well. It was only three pages and there was no doubt that it could be shortened a little bit if everything went well. The director guided himself to an empty seat while the volunteer chose the chair across from the device. Serenity was all that could be heard from the three men that sat in the shadows. Alistair, the one who was positioned at the left, had a long wispy moustache coated with white, skin, a fleshy-pink, and a pair of spectacles over jade-green eyes. Martin, the figure in the middle, wore a cap that positioned the brim to the back, orange stubble on his chin gave the impression he was young, and a pudgy nose loomed over his lips. Finally, Oscar was a Caucasian male that had long tufts of golden brown and a stone-cold reflection. Lying next to the communicator was another pair of the headsets that the silent men were wearing. The two took one each and pulled it over their heads.

"Another one of your gadgets?" a question arose from John as he pointed to one of the first headphones ever invented. Martin looked to where he was being pointed to, and nodded before going back to being hunched over a pad of paper with a ballpoint pen. He would never understand these men with their secret agendas, and it only made him wonder at what they were really doing here with Coratio and him.

"Yeah, something like that." The appointed negotiator and the director glanced at the engineer and caught him grinning ear-to-ear.

"What do you call them?" he asked again.

"Headsets, Mr. Vauge!" a curt answer was given from the director.

"Oh it was nothing, really, it was nothing. The design was rather too simple for my taste, but the simplest inventions prove to be the best." He finished speaking and it was now evident that he, and the rest of the ensemble of three weren't as secretive as he thought. Or were they?

"Anyway, I believe we should be starting. Simply press that tiny, red switch once you're ready. And of course you'll need the microphone," a tall, rectangular piece of equipment was passed on to the man who would stop change.

"You think it's too late to back out?" asked Vauge, a tone of seriousness masking its purpose.

"Now, John, you better be joking," Coratio worried.

"Yeah, I'm joking."

"False alarm, everybody; he's staying after all," the director ended the joke with one sentence. The room filled with laughter that died soon due to the clearing of a throat and the flick of a switch. The script was looked at as static filled all five of the headsets.

Then, the first sentence was sent out.

"Is anyone there?"

Silence. More silence. And then a voice was heard that was very much not alien. "Yes we're here, Dumbo." Everyone at the table now had a look of nervous awe as the Falls' spokesperson with his British accent retorted. Ever since the Fallokratists had floated about in Earth's atmosphere, they had learnt the truth, the British were aliens, or at least some of them were. "And yes we know, we're idiots, bullies, and British. Of course, not all of us are British. We have everything from Scots to New Yorkans. We are also, as you say, a diverse alien race. Which, now come to think of it, you probably don't say that at all. Now, if you have a problem with this, please call nine-nine-nine; leave us alone. Goodbye."

"No, wait," the script left John's hands and ended up on the carpeted floor, while Oscar snuffed out his cigarette in the nearby ashtray.

"Wait! No, I will not wait. Waiting is for waiters. Hah! Get it human? Wait, waiters," a roar of laughter rang from the communicator.

"Yes, I get it. At least, aliens know how to joke," John murmured under his breath.

"Hey, what's that supposed to mean? Besides, that's racist; I'm not an alien. I'm British."

"I know you are. But I have an important question that can't wait."

"It's not important and I already know it."

"If you know what I'm going to ask you, what's the answer?"

Without hesitation the British Fall replied, "No."

"Why? Is it wrong to ask another species a favor? Especially if it's a noble species I ask it to?" The other members at the table gave warnings with their eyes in the form of glares. He answered them with an, "I know what I'm doing" gesture.

"Hmm, what a good point, human. Noble, I like the sound of that. Wait just a moment. Jimmy, what do I say? He called us noble. Oh alright, if you say so. Well, my boss just informed us that we're not noble at all. We're actually the filthiest bunch you'll ever see. I mean here, of course."

Vauge could make out the faint drawl of a Texan Fall in the background. It would seem from this that the Falls were multi-accented and had sections on their planet like the humans did.

But having no desire to know about this, John never asked. "So that means no favors."

"Nope!"

"At all?"

"Nope!"

"So that means you will do us a favor?"

"No, we will absolutely not grant favors to peasants."

"I see. How about a bribe? Do you like bribes?"

The question made the men around the table uneasy but they all knew it was worth it.

"Definitely not! I mean, yes, we do. What do you have in mind, human?"

"Perhaps in return for our good old selves we could give you an earth treasure."

"Treasure, I do like the sound of that. Wait just one moment. Jimmy!" the alien screamed. "What do I say? He spoke of the tee word! Oh thank you, sir! Well my boss just informed me that that is indeed allowed."

Vauge smiled to himself, "Good. Is there anything in particular you have in mind?"

"Why yes. In fact, we want only one thing. One small thing. One very small thing. So small that you'll never even miss it. We would like this painting you call Mona Lisa."

Everyone in the room became still. And the only thing that broke the serenity was Coratio rapidly dialing numbers into a telephone. He then spoke hurriedly before putting the phone back into its rightful spot.

"Tell the Fall you're arranging his order," the director whispered behind his left hand.

"Hello?" the British Fall called out from the communicator.

"Umm, I'm back but I'll have to end this transmission; otherwise your delivery may not be ready until it's too late."

"What's that supposed to mean? You're not planning anything that I wouldn't do, are you?"

"No, absolutely not," and with that, the switch was flicked and the voice was silenced.

Vauge followed director Coratio out through the open door and into an almost-empty hallway. "That couldn't have gotten any worse," Coratio blurted out with balled fists.

"You ordered a fake, didn't you?"

"Of course, I did. You think I would give them the real thing?"

"Absolutely not! But do we know if we can get one today?"

Coratio stopped in his tracks, "It'll be here in an hour or less. And so far we have no news about the missile," he said and checked his watch. "It's mere seconds from ten, Vauge."

"We wait then," Vauge sat down at a bench propped against the wall.

"I'd like to think there's another option."

A phone rang from inside the recently exited room and Coratio went in to join it. The telephone adjacent to the communication setup was picked up. "Are you serious? They're doing it now? I thought we had more time. We had an agreement. You backstabber! Okay, I'll get back to you."

He exited and sat down next to his old friend. "The rebels just fired the missile from a base in Canada."

"Well, then we'll have to find another way," he sighed as he was being watched by the director. Next thing the two knew they were sitting around the table again and Vauge placed the headset firmly on his coated head. The setup was turned on, "Hey! I'm back."

“It took you long enough. So is the Mona Lisa gonna get shipped to us or not?”

“I’m afraid that’s not possible, Fall.”

“The name’s Tom and what do you mean, not possible?”

“I mean, you have to go, now! There’s a class B missile headed for your ship.”

“Do you mean to say that earth is gonna try to destroy the Falls, with one of your puny weapons? You coward! You should’ve never tried reversing our experiment.” All sound turned back to its original static and everyone in the room knew that the alien vessel had left its orbit around earth. They had succeeded with saving the Falls from an end that would’ve haunted them for a very long time. But in truth, had they really succeeded? Was everything back to normal? Coratio was on the phone again and everyone had an uneasy smile fastened to their jaws. The director got off his call.

A long pause was enacted before he spoke, “I’m very happy to announce that the missile blew up in empty space. As for the whole experiment on us humans, it’s been reported that everything is seemingly back to how it should be.” Clapping ensued but John Vauge stood in silent victory. Everything was how it should be and it was thanks to him for warning the Falls of their possible destruction. I guess they had decided that he wasn’t a coward after all. And maybe the Falls weren’t that bad after all either. But there was still a chance they would return to earth. But what would happen then?

THE END-1

After a minute of thought, Vauge decided what he was going to say, "Sorry, Coratio, but I'm going to have to decline." And he stood up.

"Decline! Are you absolutely sure?" the director almost shouted.

"I am, yes. When they said I was done with saving the world from terrorists, and now aliens, they meant it. Goodbye, Alvin."

Director Alvin Coratio was now standing alone in the dark, mouth wide-open. He picked up the telephone from his desk and dialed in a string of numbers.

"Umm, hello! We have a problem. That's right, he said no. Yes, I realize what that means. Okay, goodbye," Coratio said

The phone was set down. "Life will never be the same again," Coratio murmured to himself.

The elevator closed and John was almost out the lobby door when he had a notion to go and see how the secretary, Jessica, was doing. "That was your fault back there. I would've never said no," he said and leaned against the counter.

The lady stopped typing and turned to him with a smirk. "I gave them a choice and this is the alternative they chose. But if you have to blame an existent source, yes, just blame me. After all, I am the author!"

"Hah! That's what you say. But I still doomed the world and it's not my fault." He was closer to the door now and he hesitated before compelling himself to forget what the day had brought. This was all a dream; it had to be. He left the building and Jessica went back to chiseling out Vauge's life on the fateful day of November 25, 1965. That was the day the change decided to stay.

Fifty-four years later, on November 25, 2019, the worldwide incident was still known as the day the humans blew up their problem. Of course, blowing up the Falls never worked, and neither did the Jeong serum. The serum, instead, did nothing at all and only caused the humans to grumble about their predicament. This changed overtime when they realized they had to adapt to their new life. And it also meant that everything that had been built had to be changed. In other words, everything had been messed up and augmented. Ordinary life was now different from how it had been. Even John Vauge, the world's worst failure, had come to accept fate. He was now married and had two kids. One was thirty-one and approximately five feet while the other was forty-three and almost four feet. But that was nothing compared to how tall John was. He was eighty-two and had been twenty-eight in 1965, which meant he was exactly three feet and eighty inches. His wife Claudia, on the other hand, was eighty-one and only three feet and sixty inches. So yes, life was not the same and it would never be how it was in '65. This was how it would be until the end of the world. And nothing could change that, or at least, that's what they thought.

THE END-2

0IIIII2000000000:

THE PURPLE DOT
1

A serpentine world floated aimlessly in the darkness of space. It was fulfilling what it had been created to do, design a world suitable for humans. And the only reason it did this was because on the last day of earth, a doctor by the name of Henry Wigget, invented a planet that could build itself. It had been designed to keep life and to give the human race a new world to be sustained on. So he uploaded himself into the system and when the rocket containing the artificial world was sent into space, it started doing what it had been programmed to do. It was carving a planet out of the ruins of its carrier. In that very moment, that was all there was. Then, over a period of days, it finished shaping the ball of dirt. But before it got a chance to put living beings on it, an unknown piece of matter was encountered. This insignificant chunk was too close for comfort as it sped, heading for the world. It was swallowed whole as the planet defended itself. Matter or not, the virus had been multicoloured and had tried uselessly to swarm and attack its prey. The fight continued as the original blueprint was mutated and the very first human it created was not a human at all. Instead, it formed a grey pair of hands entwined at the wrists like a statue. It wasn't long before the hands were filled to the brim with a bubbling liquid. An orange essence it held that could've been described as having the properties of carrot juice. Perhaps it was exactly that, or maybe it was extraterrestrial and therefore something else. This was a humor to something that didn't understand the word. The orange substance suddenly glowed brightly from the deep with an ember light that floated towards the surface. It was soon extinguished like a fire waiting to be blown out, only for it to resume its course with success. The ember light stretched out a thin hand from beneath the juice. Behold the sight for then a form crawled out with arms that lurched out for something to hold on to. It was a blob, then a spot. And finally when it had come to an agreement with itself, it was more like a dot. The world of block had just artistically woven its first man-like being. He stood up to full height and from the view of a set of triangle-eyes, he perceived the world he was given. The things he saw amazed him like the oceans of snaking blue and the range of pointy mountains that lined the outskirts of a city. This was the first time he had seen beauty, and so he spoke to himself like no one else was there.

"I look at this world I find myself in. I am the first and I have just begun what I know to be life. Here I am, standing at the edge of cold hands. I am the raindrop that has fallen to the living," he said this with a wise man's words as a tail grew from his backend. The tail instinctively curved and swayed to the sides with a fluent gesture as he looked down at his skinny, tubular arms. At the end of the two purple, twig-like arms, a circle of the same colour existed; he called them 'hands.' His legs also appeared to be sprouting from the bottom of the dot and there at the bottom of his legs were two more flat squares. The intervention of the mysterious matter had caused the first human to be nothing like its original copy. But that wasn't the important factor. What was important was that this purple dot had the consciousness of Dr.Henry Wigget. The only thought Dr. Wigget possessed at this point was the question on how this could be reversed. And he had to find it, with his new body. He had been reborn with a quest that was surging through his very mind. But the only entity that knew the cause was Block. The creator had to find a way to reach out to his creation. He had to speak to a planet that couldn't reply. Not just that; the planet was growing and becoming more sophisticated by the second. The only solution would be buried by the detail and there would be no way of reversing the glitch. He jumped from the hands and landed firmly on more rock. All around him the world was twisting, building more of him in order to have an idea on what a human civilization looked like. The Purple Dot peered over the rock edge and looked into the gaping mouth that an ocean had left behind. It was a wormhole where water fell through and this, the dot knew to be the weak spot. It started closing, sensing that the Purple Dot was about to rebel against its new programming. However, before it could close entirely, Dr.Henry Wigget disappeared into it with a fall. Time passed, which would have been characterized as a day. Then finally, a purple hand appeared and with it a purple dot. He pulled himself to the edge of the waterfall and stood there with a look that meant everything would be all right. Or would it? He began his climb to the top of the mountain where his home resided. Once he got to the top he planned to sit at his birth place and watch a civilization form and then fall. He was filled with nothing now to occupy himself but to watch earth multiply in population. But as he began to sit down he noticed something from a distance away. His wait was now for two things, rather than one. He scrunched up his eyes to let through a blob of grey, so he sat down and began the wait. A wait that he hoped would end well. A wait that would result in an encounter and a fascination in life. But like the worrisome and curious person he was, he also had a small sliver of doubt. However, in the meantime, why don't I tell you about what happened with his mission in the watery abyss?

2

The Purple Dot fell down a void of cold, blue water before changing to a swim. And then as quickly as the submerging had begun, it ended. It ended and he found himself in a cavern. Having no desire to stay in the freezing body of water, he frantically searched for land. Then, when he spotted a dry-sand beach, a few long strides took him to shore. Lying there on the sand, he pulled himself onto his bare feet. Not before glimpsing a silvery arch before him. One thing was certain; it didn't match with the rest of the scenery. It didn't belong with the stone walls and old atmosphere that took a living in the underwater cavern. Dr.Henry Wigget took a step forward that could never make it past the archway. There was a trap waiting for him that had been set by the planet. It was possessed by the alien entity and now it was keeping survival at its peak interest. Its misguided peak. The sand around the arch activated its defense system as it stood on its hind legs. Or rather the two creatures that had been lying underneath the sand did. It happened quickly and caught Dr.Wigget off guard but he was soon ready to overcome Block's misguided defense. There, in front of him, were two hounds that he knew were really enlarged copies of what earth's dog should have looked like. The reptilian-green eyes mixed with the dark, furred body, was a bad dream to Dr.Wigget. He dodged a pounce from one of them but only to be thrown to the rough, sandy ground from the other. Luckily, to make a short story shorter, he found a bone. He was lying on the sand, the hounds growling and breathing unpleasant air into his face, while he scavenged with both hands in the sand. If the contaminated planet could treat him like an enemy, there was a chance that a part of it would try to protect him. The hounds' eyes glowed as they pawed and bared their teeth threateningly. But before they could attack, Dr. Wigget's hands found what he was looking for. There, covered in a layer of sand, was a femur belonging to a rather tall bipedal. A smile crept onto the dot's face as the tidbit of chance was fulfilled. He took this as a sign that the planet's AI was still there. That hope was still there; he could get it back, he knew it. Dr.Wigget grasped the bone in his right hand before it was hurled across the small beach and into the body of water with a splash. The hounds leapt for joy at the sight of a new victim as the Purple Dot congratulated himself. Then, he put a palm out on the granules of the beach, congratulating Block. The archway joined him as he ran for it, branching off into a tunnel that trailed downward. All the dim light he had had was now being suffocated as the tunnel became darker and darker. Which wasn't as painless now that there was an intruder at large. At some point, he had fallen down several steps and that only made him want to get to the rocket even sooner than before. He finished descending into the innards of Block, and had started losing a shred of hope over the long journey as a blip of light cut through the dark. At this point, he had two goals that seemed further from success than ever. (1) Get to the rocket, and (2) stop the virus that plagued Block. He gave up as he heavily sat down on the stone floor. Only to sit up with a torch in hand. "Thank you, Block. You're trying to tick the intruder out. And you're doing good, creation. I'm proud of you," he whispered.

The Purple Dot furthered until the stone walls led to a door of the same shine as the arch. A hand came to it and it clicked open, only to disappoint him with another stretch of walking and another door. This happened again and again, door after door, but there was still no sign of an end. Doubt crept into his mind, telling him he would never get to the heart of a world, but he never let that stop him. Hope was what fueled him. And soon, this paid off. Finding another door at the end of the tunnel, he murmured a prayer. And seeing as time was of the essence, he tried it. And it opened. Instead of finding another tunnel he was introduced to a brightly-lit room. No longer needing the torch, he commanded it to switch off. He had found light both literally and figuratively speaking; he no longer needed an extinguishable flame. The door shut behind him and he was left all alone in the ruined rocket. And there at his side was the control panel in which the planet's consciousness resided. Therefore, this left the planet's body in the rocket and all around Dr.Wigget. The rocket was his son's brain, and he was inside it. The father's fingers splayed themselves across a messy and entangled keyboard. "Something screwed up the program. It's been drastically altered to read the human reconstruction code differently." Henry mumbled out his concern before typing out related text. "Come on, what did this?" he asked as he pressed the small shape that served as an enter. But the end result was different from the information he had been expecting.

The words, "I did," now displayed in a dark-green font. A font amongst black. A new message was displayed, this time belonging to the occupant of the question.

"Who's I?" the screen went blank but came on again with more text.

"I have no name for you to know me by. Only what I am. The Intruder; that's what you call me. If you really want to know my name, wait! That's how you can defeat me." Whatever had infected the AI was an intelligent life form, which meant that it was easier to communicate with it. The Purple Dot was excited at this new thread that had sprung from the mysterious intruder. But it also knew what it meant; it threatened the system. Dr.Wigget slowly nodded to the accurate presumption. "You nodded. Which frightens you, Doctor Wigget!" The message alarmed its receiver.

"What do you want?" he typed furiously to the next strand of letters.

"You know what I want." That was it; it was obvious what it wanted. It wanted the planet for itself. The intruder's survival depended on Block.

"Why should I hand it over?" The Intruder had merged with the planet before it had activated its anti-virus program. It was due to this that it had no defense against the mysterious malware and had therefore been unable to stop it at all. Luckily, Doctor Wigget had set in a safety measure that installed as soon as the planet had started forming. It was a restart mechanism that would erase the identity of the AI consciousness. The AI would automatically be shut down for as long as it needed to force the virus out, leaving it with nowhere to go. After getting rid of The Intruder, Dr.Wigget would have to replace the planet AI with a new consciousness, which wasn't the basic program he had created. A few commands later, he was in the very mainframe of what he'd built. Now, all he'd have to do was replace the basic with one of the chosen personality programs.

His opponent meanwhile answered the doctor, "because you have no choice. I have taken over from here. Block shall be mine. It's I that should be asked to hand it over." Dr.Wigget ignored what the computer told him for the time being. On the screen was a list that included the basic program at the topmost. And below that were several names belonging to the few humans that were elite enough to be uploaded alongside its creator. Elite, as in those who had enough money, smarts, or political power to be able to successfully grow a new economy and civilization. They would be the first humans to settle on Block. The creator scrolled down to his name, which was listed as the fourth uploaded human. With a quick decision, he chose himself to be the new AI after the basic one had been deleted. The Purple Dot would become the sole consciousness of Block. He would be the planet. The top listing was clicked and its deletion was confirmed. It disappeared from the screen and all of sudden Dr.Wigget got a dark feeling that nothing good had been achieved. A feeling that was deafened by a quake that shook the rocket. This gave him motivation to work quickly; he had only a short time to replace the consciousness before the virus could act. But before he did so, he felt a sensation that made him quiver. And in an instant, he realized what had happened. He was no longer the Purple Dot, he was his original self. With a smile on his spectacled-face and gladness that he was wearing synthesized clothing, he started the program switch. He was hovering directly above his name and ready to confirm. The only thing that held him back was a worrying feeling. What if he should think about someone else to take on the job? Maybe this was selfish of him. He adjusted his spectacles as he gazed through the list of subjects. Who would be perfect to sustain a world with their intelligence? Would it be Jessica Ortell, Samson Druedo, Arik Summers, or that familiar name at the bottom of the screen? The Purple Dot. Dr.Wigget's double identity could, he realized, be the perfect consciousness. But the thing is he was The Purple Dot. This had to be a trick. The Intruder was trying to get back into power. But the thing was—did this newborn really want to change again? Did he want to go back to something less than what he was? He looked down at his hands and thought hard about what it meant to be immortal. Did he really want to be human again? The answer, was no. The first word that came to mind was "boring." Besides, an afterlife with a different persona was bound to be audacious. But what if it was a trick? What if it was The Intruder? A name was highlighted, Arik Summers. She was an acting student at Cambridge and had several PhDs in the sciences before earth's sun died out. Earth's top board of scientists thrived to find a way to prolong death, and Dr.Wigget had helped them. He created Block before the sun went out and froze them to icicles. No one survived. He was to be the first resurrected in Block's form because of him being the creator. He was to be the first new human. A council had even been collected with the highest of the humans and they all bickered as to who the first Blockian would be.

"I want to be the first."

"No, I."

It went on until a voice rose higher than the rest. "No, Dr. Wigget was the founder of this idea. He will be the one."

The name highlighted reminded Wigget of the last moments of life. The cold burning and then nothing as he saw himself freeze.

The name highlighted, Summers, had been a friend of Henry, not to mention a valued student. He had been her physics and history professor. The name was selected without much thought, but to his surprise, an error page popped up. The file had been blocked without his knowledge of it.

"What the…!" he exclaimed. In a flash, this wasn't all as every name, except his and the Purple Dot, darkened to match the background of black. This was a trap, a game that the virus was playing. It had somehow survived its deletion and now it was ensuring its dominance. With one of the two programs selected, the virus would become Block. Or he had set it up so that the creator had a fifty-fifty chance of eliminating him. And what if after this, he forever became the Purple Dot? He scanned both of the choices again. He would go with his gut and play the reverse-psychology card. Assuming the virus knew that he was going to choose himself but also felt that he was better as the Purple Dot, the virus would choose Dr.Henry Wigget. But what if it already knew that he'd choose himself and deliberately hid his control in the Purple Dot? Using this logic, Dr.Wigget picked the purple alter-ego as his new body. The planet rumbled back to life from its seconds of dormancy. He had become the Purple Dot once more, and gulped. Didn't the virus create this alternate version of the human? So was it possible that he had fallen to the Intruder's will? Did it mean that the doctor had just endangered his life and planet? No! The Purple Dot disagreed with this due to the scan he had done prior to him choosing. Before, when he had gone over the names, he had run a diagnostic scan over every program on the console. According to the scan, Block was virus-free. Sighing, he reassured himself. The Intruder had been dissipated. Besides, now that he was the Purple Dot again, the last moments on earth were gone from his memory. He didn't even remember a single thing. Block now had Doctor Henry Wigget's persona and consciousness. So with everything back to how it should have been the system was shut down for the time being. The Purple Dot started his travel back to the surface. He had found light by supposedly stopping a threat and discovering a revelation of himself. He was lying to himself about being in control. The same way he had almost lost a planet, he had lost everything that kept his life together. He wasn't in control at all. On earth, he had been struggling with alcoholism, but now that was gone. Now with a grim smile, he could finally put his life back together. To him, 'Finding Light,' was a second chance. Another chance in the millions he had been countlessly given. And now that he had been given the ultimate second chance, he would try his utmost hardest to fulfill it. Do something that mattered, instead of making himself miserable. The world of Block was a good outlet for this. It had been freed from the one day invasion on its mind. And it needed a watchful protector. Nonetheless, the words of the Intruder stayed, "If you really want to know my name, wait!" He doubted that the virus could ever come back. But it was a great idea, Dr.Wigget thought. Waiting for a return that would never happen, kinda prove the virus wrong, while being a protector for his new earth. He left as the console turned on, and the conversation between the two sentient continued.

"I'm still here, Doctor Henry Wigget!"

3

The Purple Dot waited and waited. Over time, the city that had been built grew until it reached from one side of the world to the other. Instead of the weariness of sitting there all this time, there was a glint in his eyes and a smile abroad his lips. He had never moved from that sitting spot that he had taken so long ago. He could've if he wanted to, but he didn't because he was afraid that maybe he would miss something. Dr.Henry Wigget felt like a father to a newly spun infant. Particularly, not just an infant but instead, a swarm of colourful ants that he could tell were working hard to make him proud. Somewhere in there, his friends, Arik Summers and company, were part of the chaotic building of Block. This was why the idea of missing one detail of Block's superior race suddenly terrified him so much. So much that he wished to be forever frozen in one spot. The Purple Dot sat there on the top of the mountain like a piece of art being shown at an exhibit, and never inched a muscle. In his new form, he was capable of sitting still for dozens of years. But his old self would've been unable to do so after sometime. "Glad that you're not me?" The Purple Dot heard his earthling and deeper-toned self speak from the very center of the planet.

The cartoon Mr.Wigget had a squeakier and less deep voice. "Yeah, kinda," the Purple Dot chuckled back. The smudge of grey in the distance had gotten clearer now. But still he waited for an answer to all the speculations he had on the slowly arriving figure. "Do you know who the gray blob is?"

"I have my suspicions, and you have your suspicions. But what do you think?" The AI changed the topic.

"I don't know. I have a sneaking fear, AI me. It can be either a friend or foe. Especially now with the Intruder gone, I don't really know who it could be. Except...," he paused, "maybe it's Jessica. Or some other program. The virus did let go of the installed consciousness after I banished him to the deepest of space."

"What is this fear you have then, son?" the voice passed across the top of the mountain. The stone hands from the Purple Dot's first day stood in artificial cobwebs. The spot in the distance grew into a small shape very recognizable to him. That didn't say it wasn't surprising at all to the waiting dot.

"Oh, you know what I fear. It coming back. It won't though; it won't," the dot let his body down on the rock close by. The Purple Dot was now in an old age of seven-hundred and had discovered that immortality could get dull. He knew that from the beginning when he took on the job as a watcher. His life was driven only to see who was advancing toward him. The first creation believed that this had to be first before meeting his kin in the city. But that wouldn't happen for a long time.

"I do, Son. I don't know why I call you son; you are me. We are one and the same but different in bodies. I have none, and you are a fictional character." The planet answered back with a bit of poet's zest.

"I guess so. Can't disagree with you, big Dad! The way I see it, we may be the same, but you're most definitely the old guy from Pinocchio," the dot relaxed with a grin and arms behind his body.

"And you're Pinocchio, I gather?"

"You better believe it!" the son exclaimed.

"Do you fully understand that without you they would be cartoon characters? Yes, cartoons are all good, but that's not our real image. We are made in the image of greatness."

"Like I've known. I took the sacrifice for them. Became that which they didn't want to become. And come to think of it, seems funny now that you're the human part of me, and I'm the inhuman part. Because sometimes it feels like it's way too good to be true. A perfect life feels way too far away to take hold. 'Cause the truth is I doubt. Humans doubt way too much. And I wish we could make these...," the Purple Dot motioned to the civilization far down. He didn't know it but some would look up and from far off they would see a vague outline of a mountain. They would see nothing of him. They didn't know he existed, didn't know that another earth had once been a thing. And, of course, they wouldn't know that they were new beings on a new world. Some of them over time told stories about the mountain and their belief that their creator sat atop it, but didn't fully take in what this meant. Others thought this was make-belief and had their own stories. But even some took nothing of anything. They didn't believe in any creator. Earth was alive in Block's people when it came to belief, and that was for sure. They were living day-to-day lives like the old humans would've and they didn't even know it. It was just their ways and the adaptations they believed took place on the way. Like on old earth, they thought they came from primitives. In a way, it was far superior being born on Block than being born on earth, so this was an adequate assumption. "...At least a little better," the Purple Dot went on. "The things we did on earth were terrible. We destroyed everything good and the world. We polluted our minds and bodies. We tried to be good, but it's hard. It's really hard," the relaxation was gone and replaced with pure, emotional frustration. "This is another second chance. And I'm afraid it's going to get wasted." There was no answer from the planet, and the Purple Dot got worried. The original Doctor Wigget had also had a serious case of worrying since he was a tiny tot. His parents had always said it was a genetic pass-me-down from his father, and that's how it stayed. No amount of medication or self-discipline had solved his problem. It was a part of him. "Talk to me, Wigget. Please don't tell me...," he shot to his feet and glanced at the figure in the distance. It morphed before his eyes into a dot and was now in close range. The time had come to see if waiting had been worth it. And it was, but it also contained a resolute fear. The other dot's eyes burnt like the lights from the city. And as shadow fell on his face, Wigget's son found it menacingly beautiful. Mesmerized by the impossible dot that shouldn't have existed, he forgot about the planet's voice. They looked into each other's eyes in a trance. They had both been searching for a figure in the distance, and they weren't sure if curiosity was fulfilled. The dot for whom he had been waiting for, for so long, was an exact replica of himself. The only detail that was left out was that this replica had been ripped of colour. The Purple Dot wasn't disappointed at the replica for being less than he had hoped for. It did, however, fill him with anger and the same feeling of fear for his world. "You still exist!"

"How do you know who I am?" The gray dot already knew the answer.

"I've always known it even though I dismissed it. That's one of the infinitesimal reasons I stayed as the Purple Dot. If you ever came back, then I could finally meet you and stop you once and for all."

"Hmm. It wasn't in the AI code you designed, Dr. Wigget, and that's why you took it," he spoke with a slithery take on the dot's speech.

"I'm not him. I chose what you created."

"Because you, Mr. Wigget, don't want to be human. You find it boring," he sneered in jest.

"And I regret it. My talk with the Wigget AI shook up some of my senses. By the way, Intruder, where is he? Where is the planet?" the dot drew closer.

Instead of Intruder answering, a voice inhabited the planet. He was the new Block. "I ran my own measures and duplicated myself into the planet and a form that best served me. Which as it happens, isn't this one that you see," Intruder boomed from an invisible speaker.

"I'm curious, Intruder, what can I do to make an agreement with you?"

"I want your planet and I won't back down. I am unstoppable," both the gray dot and the consciousness rang out at the same time.

“I’ll take that as a no. I can’t make an agreement. And in that case, I don’t think I have much choice. You deleted my AI consciousness, or at least I presume you did.”

“I destroyed him as he screamed in desperation. He’s gone; you are now under my control, Dr.Wigget,” the Intruder was as menacing as the things he said.

“Get off my planet! And if you won’t, I will take it back. I designed Block to not just house life, but to defend against anything that threatened that life.”

“Aah, that petite little force field. What else do you have? How are you going to defeat me, creator?” the gray dot mocked.

“You’ll see! And don’t let me tell you anymore I warned you!” the Purple Dot grinned. “Activate the thermossiles! Set three on the nearest alien bio figure!” Now it was the intruder’s turn to worry as his AI was garbled out by a monotonous consciousness.

“Are you sure, Dr.Wigget?”

“Yes; activate!”

“Please no. Let me stay. I’ll be good. Let me just have my own world. Create me my own world!” he begged for freedom.

Dr.Wigget’s eyebrows arose “Wait! Deactivate the projectiles!” he tried at the hope of an agreement after all. But before the word missiles was out, a horde of fire from the other side of the planet struck the blob of gray. He backed down, hand over his eyes, as he watched the flame strike the gray dot. But when the smoke drifted away, Dr.Wigget was absolutely shocked to see that the Intruder was still standing. He was stained head to toe with burn marks, but unharmed.

“Had a change of heart, doctor? Nah! You don’t have a heart, do you?” the unscathed enemy mocked again.

Without hesitation the creator gave out a new command. “Double the damage! Six thermossiles—activate!”

“Are you really sure, sir?” The AI was hesitant.

“Yes I am. Positive… Wait, I never authorized a new AI!”

“That’s because I did.” Doctor Henry Wigget realized hope and a second chance were evading his control after so many years.

He fell in an act of emergency. “Cancel that command, now! Cancel!”

“Unfortunately,” Intruder’s consciousness became in control, “you no longer have access to Block.”

“You can’t do this. At least you’ll get what’s coming to you!” he started with defeat and ended with victory. Only to be pushed back down with defeat.

Intruder manically chuckled, “You thought you could win! You thought you could rid the pest. But not this time! This time, the pest will rid the exterminator!”

“What?”

“Don’t sound confused, creator! You forgot to include yourself; you’re an alien now! And I’m not.” The other dot gave him a strange look and then a flicker of colours passed over him. Not just any colours, but bright ones It was so bright that Wigget scrunched his eyes and then when it stopped, stared back at a vision that was definitely not him. Within a small fraction of time, the gray dot had become a human. First, it was his original self, Dr.Henry Wigget, but with a malevolent grin. And then, when that didn’t last very long, it was a fictional favorite.

"Oh no, you don't, Intruder! You're speaking to me through one of my favorite Victorian characters. Scratch that, my favorite written character! You accessed my data file."

"Which means…?"

"It means, you know everything about me. You have access to every single human on this planet."

"Incorrect, you little cartoon character!" Another menacing smile was pulled from the shapeshifting entity.

"They're all like me," he came to terms with what the other said. "They are no longer humans. You stupid virus… you have taken everything from me! Now I'm going to die. Why? Why did you do this? Why?" Frantic emotion ran through the last human of earth. He wasn't even a human anymore.

"You tried to destroy me, but you failed. And I must have Block; I must live. This body I have cursed you and the other humans with, you wanted it to stay. Remember your decision in the rocket. Now, you'll have to stay with it, for eternity. That is if I cancel the missiles."

"Please, cancel them."

"Why? Why should I cancel your execution," the soft Londoner's chime of the virus made Wigget miss his home world.

"I'll give you so much," was all he could muster.

"Give me more, creator! Give me, Block!" the virus demanded.

Dr.Wigget shook his head and then bit his lip, "No! I will not!"

Standing in front of Henry, was a man who wore a light-brown deerstalker on the very top of his black-haired crown. His face was elegantly trimmed and was drawn in with a mixture between pale and light-pink skin. Of course, the monotony of gray soon flickered back and then went. Below the virus' nose were pipe-clenched lips. And there at the end of the mahogany pipe where small curls of grey smoke billowed, was his right hand. Alas! The final major detail was a coat made of pure Irish wool upon his frame.

"Then goodbye, Purple Dot!"

As the detective said this, the next horde of missiles bore down on the creator and pummeled him with fire. And like before when the smoke cleared, he was still standing. The virus was outraged, "How is this possible? I relinquished all of your control. Block is mine."

"I admit you did," the dot started with a frown, "but I guess I had a tidbit of control left. Faith and hope, Intruder. They go a long way, you know. You should try them sometime."

"I still have more control than you do. You might still be alive, creator. But I can always get rid of you in other ways." But before Wigget could step closer, he was stopped mid-stride by the man with the pipe.

"I won't stop till you're gone. No matter what!" the used-to-be human promised.

"Then, I wouldn't step closer if I were you," warned the virus.

"Why? Why shouldn't I?" Wigget dared.

"Because, Mr. Wigget, you'll never stop me. You don't even know what's going to happen next. Once this planet, Block, is fully mine, I will do so much with it. It has an AI. Not only that; it's also the first AI planet in the whole entire galaxy and there's so much I can do with it," he reveled in the imaginary power he could have.

"We'll see about that! I am Henry Wigget and Block doesn't belong to you, he declared urgently with veracity.

"And the first thing I'm going to do, Wigget…," Intruder said, ignoring the puny obstacle, "is delete you from existence."

The final straw had been pulled for Wigget; he had to act now.

"You will absolutely do no such thing. You will not lock me out from my own creation. I'll make sure of that." He wore a smile as he stepped forward, not heeding the warning that had been set. All he cared about was the survival of his planet and there was no way he would let someone else take it from him. But the one thing he should've considered before stepping further was whether there was any ground to support him. He had been on top of the mountain where he had been born and had just barely been lured off the edge.

The one who had lured him shook his head, "Tut, tut; what an ignorant one he was. Boy, am I going to enjoy taking all of this for my own. Muah, hahaha. Hope I never see you again, Purple Dot!"

This was his second fall as he lost another chance to fix the misfortune in his life. The addictions and the oh-so-many regrets he had had as a human. But the only way to really change the time he had uselessly spent he had to make it up by saving a whole civilization. And the only way to do that was with the fall. Unlike the first one, this was the real journey. He would have to climb up once again and then there was the problem with Block. It wasn't his anymore.

THE FEAST
PART 1-THE MORG RACE

On the planet Morg, the annual festival of Yartav approached full velocity. The name Yartav came from a native of our history who had been banished for killing the king in that era. It was a scandal. More in fact it was a framing. Or at least I believe it was a framing. Yartav Baskov, was a son to King Baskov and like some stories, they hated each other. Their guts included. In the end, Yartav slayed the dragon and became the king. He is to this day the king, a great king. And that's why every year, as humans call it, we celebrate. For our living king and the king in the skies still have full reign. For the celebration, everyone had prepared by procuring a variety of foods, talents, and creativity-fueled projects. But those who had not an eye for such hobbies prepared themselves for an athletic game that makes them competitors. An athletic game we Morgians called the Morg race. The great Morg race never stayed the same; it always changed. This is what lured the champions to the prized competition, an unlimited way of playing it. It brought anyone, not just us, together to compete for a prize. Unlimited knowledge, that's what the prize was. How the officials of Morg had access to this, no one knows, but faith has been placed in the minds of everyone, especially the competitors. It is seen as god given. They lap up whatever the officials of Morg say, processing everything as the truth. More on the race, the commentators, or the people who ran the game, decided on the obstacles and the scenery. They are the challengers, and the competitors, the challenged. My focus for the race will be on a fellow Morgian. Let me introduce one of the competitors, a personal friend of mine, Table. Now, this was finally his time to participate in the Morg race because you only get one chance to be either a victor or a loser. It's even a rare chance to be in it. Of course, when you lose in the game you disappear, but he simply thought this to be something less than death. You get transported to the other side of the planet and a participation package is then given; that's what happens. Or that's what he said last time we talked as friends.

The nervousness mixed with adrenaline, and then he knew it was time. Doors opened to look out over a stadium that would eventually change with a flicker. He wasn't the only one. There, around him, were a dozen other characters in a jumble of different hairstyles and garments. None of these characters were even Morgians because my species had one trait that never got mistaken. It had never been used again to mine or Table's knowledge. We Morgians had no hair whatsoever. Everyone had a bald head and there was no way to cover it. We used to be able to wear wigs for a very short time before it was banned; apparently, we had to embrace the uniqueness. This year, in 19001, they had been disqualified from being worn. But like all rules, it was being broken on a daily basis. In the group of competitors, Table noticed multiple different races that came from completely different galaxies such as the Tralaxies. This particular species were known for their one trait, a yellow, emoji-face. The other species included: a Cor, Peel, an Ancient, Lox, and the blue-faced being known as a Rosian. It was hard to describe all of them, but I can say that each had their own attribute to share. The Rosians had fins instead of ears, cors had grey faces that led to spiky hair, and the Ancients owned coppery bodies and cold personas. The rest of the aliens' traits were the Peels' unique make-up that made them look a lot like gigantic corn cobs, and the Lox, who were born without legs and therefore used detachable limbs. The group turned heads upward to see the three commentators perched in their luxurious seats. To be exact, they floated above in serenity. The first was a middle-aged human that had hair of no colour and the second was a female with light-pink hair and skin a cool blue. Finally, the third was a native of the planet, another male, who had sparkling-green eyes and a formal wear consisting of a bright tie, a jet-black jacket, and the rest—colours that bridged the two. These commentators had always stayed the same three people. And honestly, Table doubted they would ever change. Before he was actually in the race, he had studied the game and remembered the threes' names in case he would ever become a racer. Table had had a shred of doubt that he would ever get into the competition, but with one application, he was in. That wasn't all it took. Besides the test of worthiness, there was a large fee of four-hundred tralags, which in Canadian dollars is exactly four-thousand dollars. The fee had been raised from working in the diamond mines, with a rare occurrence of finding small jobs in the marketplace. Thought was disturbed as the first commentator, Atticus, boomed into the microphone positioned in front of him. "Who's ready for a game that will challenge your wit, your puzzle-solving skills, and your athletic talent?" The assortment of players screamed in unison with several translations mixed in, not to mention that the audience jumped up from their gray benches and cheered with positive excitement. I, being in the audience, did so as well. I was rooting for Table. This was his chance, and I was hoping it went well. "That's a yes to me. How about you, Kora?" You could tell by the smile that Atticus gave that the three commentators were very good friends behind the competition. They had gone to the same academy together, basically doing everything with each other, and I know, because I was there. I wasn't a close friend, but I knew them; I went to the same academy.

"I think so, yeah," the female of the trio participated in the introduction and broke my visions of the past.

"Hey! What about me? Because it's for sure a yes," the Morgian commentator joined in.

"We didn't forget about you, Fringe. We were just trying to ignore you," Atticus retorted teasingly back.

"Wow! Very funny," the third replied. The audience roared with laughter, leaving Table unable to laugh due to nervousness. I, on the other hand, stifled back laughter, leaving a slight grin. The time was soon for everything to engulf itself in a pandemonium of action. And just then, the lead judge howled out the mention of pistol fire.

"Is there anything else, Kora, which needs to be discussed?"

"No Atticus, I think the time has come to start what we came here for." This is all very rushed; I criticized the desire for action and violence from my own shared grey bench.

"Then without further talk, may the game begin!" His words were blended into the clash of low-pitched, alien gunfire until it was no longer perceived by ears. The platform lowered its load five feet into nothingness. However, it didn't stay like that for long as the scenery was made known. What could be called scenery was a room of glass. Seven doors made the spectacle of clear material more than a three-sided zone. Six of the seven players automatically ran for a door. Once each had entered one, the final door was left, ready to be used. The other players had melted into their surroundings but this was an oblivious sight to Table. Sinking into the fabric of your environment was something impossible not to do on Morg. Once you reached the age of thirteen or were granted your twelfth ring, you would have the genetic power to melt through solids. Each couple of years every Morgian was given a test according to their profession. For each test completed successfully, they would achieve a glowing ring of whatever colour represented the difficulty of the test. Before I tell you about Table and the last door, I must describe the positioning of these doors to how he saw them, how I saw them. There were two on the left and right, three in front, and both door three and five were gone. Doors three to five were positioned in front, leaving the rest in numerical order.

"Is this a riddle?" the last competitor, Table, mumbled to himself as it quietly ricocheted off of the walls of the stadium. The question was accompanied by a sudden urge to propel himself at a wall in desperation of finding a new exit. Or at least we would find out very quickly. The easy way out was never a way to win, it was a trap set to fool the mindless. And Table knew most of all he wasn't mindless. He was smarter than that; all those years by his side proved this. Movement was directed at the door adjacent to the recently used egress. The last competitor's speed increased as he came closer to his reinstated destination. The idea of heading for the final exit was out of the question. With one giant leap, the contestant sent himself through the bridging corner between doors five and six. The audience came to the rescue with a loud gasp, one I didn't share, but as Kora stole with her own words.

"It seems that competitor number seven has broken a rule of logic. He's created his own reality, narrowly avoiding the endless pit of doom. And… jumping through a wall."

"While he's done that, competitor number six has found the unlucky door, door number one," Fringe added.

"Which means to us, Fringe, that he's found the shark tank. Munch, munch, munch… hahaha! That's one down, six to go, and a winner to be found in the end." The obnoxious sound of Atticus speaking drowned the crowd into serenity. Serenity that Table paid no attention to as he landed on a moving object. He was now number six and the second part of the competition had arrived. Looking down at the movement below his feet, he had a painting of his surroundings. This was an earthen vessel, called a train. And that fleeting darkness around him was the tunnel in which it was traveling through. The object of this challenge, I presumed he theorized, was to get from Point A to Point B, and just then it was revealed by Kora as correct.

"For the next challenge, each competitor must get to the first cabin at the very front of what is called a train. That's not all as time is of the essence and the only way out is through a portal that closes in a matter of minutes. And remember, audience, this is a game, with no rules, and someone will lose, I promise you that."

The audience cheered again as Table blindly surveyed the darkness that swallowed the stadium whole. He had two decisions, either jump across a string of roofs' never still, or creep across the train from the inside, until the cabin was found. The thing was… there was a good chance the others' would have chosen the latter. Table picked the first. Pulling back, the Morgian sprang forward like a spring. It was a bit like the pulling of a trigger that released an air-cutting projectile. Except, there was no visible target to strike. He had left one of the train boxes, leaving five smaller ones behind, but he didn't know that. With a guess, he estimated less than ten, and he was correct. Actually it was I that was correct; I saw the wide expanse of what he would have to overcome. Feeling the force of impact his feet made against the hull of the cover, he knew he'd made it. For the second time the air was pulled back behind him. Then, with a flinging of arms, he hurled himself at the dark. And missed. Arms shot out, clinging onto an edge that determined his survival.[3]Perhaps it's man that makes fate, not fate that makes man. *Ooh, I love that; I should write that in my book*, I thoughtfully played on the tip of my tongue.

Strength allowed the Morgian to haul this body gifted to him, over the edge of his problem. A body gifted by his god, for whom he did not believe in. Though he should have, for I did. And he was the almighty Thero, not a god. There below, where he'd been dangling, was the fleeting image of the tracks. And as it sped in a blur of wheels, there was one detail of the tracks that wasn't supposed to be there. He had missed a prosthetic leg. The Lox, with his disability, had lost a limb. As I sat there watching, I knew another had lost. Table made it to the next coach and so far, all was going well. Even the audience sat on the edges of their seats, anticipation written on their brows. Table's jump was repeated one more time before the

---

3 An idea on the power of man. This question can be rephrased to man making life, life making man.

darkness of the passage was replaced for the light of the day. The sun peeked out, and the more Table stared at it the more it looked like a real, live painting. The sun had been constructed with reds, yellows, and a vibrant tint of orange. It was watching over the countryside of grass and simple flocks of civilization. Too bad this wasn't actually real, Table thought as he broke the hypnotic trance. If he was me, I would be thinking that, and I don't really know if he thought that or not. After all, I can't read minds. There were two more carriages left and time wasn't to be wasted in a game where somebody could lose. On the carriage in front, a Tralaxie made a leap that almost sent him off the edge. But before he could fall, Table landed on both feet before stretching out his pale arm. The other was dragged up beside his rescuer, nodding with a grin that chilled the Morgian's bones. The game had been risked by a humane action, resulting in the crowd booing. I didn't, and was left out while I sighed. This didn't affect the pair as they shook it off and continued to the last carriage. They were now exactly where they were supposed to be. A question remained nonetheless on how they were to get in. Scratch that off' they knew how. The emoji-faced stranger lowered himself off the roof, causing his follower to delve after. It almost seemed to him that his fellow player was creating another instance for rescuing. But this wasn't the case as the audience watched in awe. A window was, instead, opened and the skinny, jacketed humanoid slipped through. Table followed behind, doing exactly the same till he was standing in a well-furnished room. A place for the waiting and a place for their belongings. To either side was a bench that would stay unused, no rest was to be given. Remember the Tralaxie? He should've never been saved. A bulky fist was thrown at the newcomer, square in the jaw. He fell to the ground with a thump and the Tralaxie made steps to leave the compartment. That never happened. As he was about to leave, he received a tap on the shoulder. One look behind him turned the tables of the fight. With a swift punch to the gut the leaving opponent reeled forward only to strike out with an elbow. The attack was then parried as Table caught it, giving the other a chance at kicking. This now left the one closer to the window at a disadvantage that was soon taken. With a quick cranium-to-cranium the struggle went back down to its original conclusion.

"You should've never rescued me, fool! Now you'll feel what it means to lose the game," the Tralaxie dragged his stunned victim to the open window. The audience cheered as I nervously rooted for Table. The Tralaxie propped him against the window to later push him out. 'Later' was now, and he readied himself to act. But instead, the stunned victim quickly recovered and shot out a punch that left him with a bloody nose. Clammy hands covered the small bump of his nose as he came to terms on what had just transpired. His stunned opponent had just given him a piece of his own medicine.

Another attack from the Morgian sent another shot at the Tralaxie's neck. Now, that was an agony that sent him wailing whilst he held a hand to his bleeding nose. "You stupid son of a...," the fallen figure started.

Bending down slightly and away from the window, the other put a finger against his lips. "Shh, this is a story for families, no swearing permitted." The audience went back to a usual booing, which angered the fallen competitor and so he got up to a stand. With a lunge that never reached the source of his rage, he got up again and stepped a little further. Once he was close to the bald stranger, it was already too late to stop. The thing that made this worse was that the target before him had just stepped aside. The Tralaxie soared through the opening and vanished from his victor's eyes. The audience reacted with grimace, which I shared. Nevertheless, Table had no time for guilt as words were made clear.

"Warning, portal to the next level evaporates in twelve seconds!" Toren announced. As soon as this was heard, speed coursed through the competitor's veins, driving him through the doorway to his left. He then instinctively went to the door across, which was labelled with a large, inky one. With his own ability of force it was opened. The handle was pulled and a blinding light lashed out at my friend's eyes and the eyes of the watching. Then it was gone in a flash. It had been darkened by the sight of nothing. A commentator spoke.

"And so, two more competitors have won the losing side of the game," Kora stole Atticus' line.

Due to this, he finished what she had started with his own words. "Player number one discovered that being crushed by a train is no ride. On the other limb, player five tasted a little bit of his own medicine."

Kora returned. "Now that leaves us with player two taking over as one, three as two, four as three, and six as four. And good luck, for I must remind thee that the reward for winning is knowledge greater than any other." The crowd cheered as Table opened his eyes to task three. Everything around him was made of dark-tinted, stone blocks. Which meant he could only be in a place known to be ancient, and very dark. And although there was only a dim film of light, the walls were seen drawing off into separate paths. To either side was a corridor, but Table took a chance with the right one. As he discovered, it turned sharply right once again and then split into four more sections. It was now evidently a labyrinth that the last participants had been dropped into. And the way to get past the third, and final challenge, was to find the way out. This would also mean that they would be at each other's throat, assuring victory for each competitor. Number three continued through the giant maze as it got darker and the faint trickle of rushing water grew louder. If that wasn't all, the walls ended, leaving a room to emerge. It was an ordinary example of the labyrinth, except cracks littered the material in an even greater show of age. Apart from the years represented here, a small fountain sat at the far wall. It flowed steadily into a pool that stayed in its boundaries. And at the other end was a doorway leading into another part of the underground world. The world of endless passages. Table's attention was otherwise focused on the bent back of the Rosian. His hands were cupped and his mouth was at company with the light-blue liquid. It was the perfect time to sneak behind the figure unnoticed. The Morgian's footsteps would be unheard by the drinking competitor. Then when he was in close proximity, he would do something that even he could never forgive. Most of all, I would never forgive him, but he would be forgiven by what he didn't believe in. The plan was set into action. His hands pushed the distracted opponent under the pool of water. And it didn't go as he had planned. Instead of going under, the stranger flipped himself over, sending his attacker stumbling. The Rosian pulled a miniature blade from his tunic, leaving the other heading for the opening. Not before, another fight began. A handful of punches, swipes, and parries were traded. It wouldn't be truthful if I said there wasn't a victor. But by the time the blade was lying on the cold ground in two pieces, the two had their share of bruises and cuts. At some point in the fight, Table had caught the blade in a swing, thrown it to the cobblestone floor, and stomped on it till it broke. It was now the Rosian's turn to head for the obvious way out. He doubled past the arch into the next section of the maze while being followed. The game of cat and mouse had begun. And several right, and left turns later, they had lost sight of each other. The Morgian adapted a caution with every step, but still doubted being sneaked upon. Boy was he wrong, and I felt worried and really crossed fingers for Table to succeed. A slithering voice like that of a snake's whispered from behind. It was more than that; it was closely behind.

So close that he felt moist lips touching the very edge of his ear… "This is for breaking my knife, punk!" he spat in his native language as it was translated. Deciphered by an invisible translator in the stadium. The mouse spun around uselessly, being unable to stop the sharp pain. I closed my eyes as the audience cheered on. I realized it was far too late. Table was going to leave the game. Therefore, his fate was left in the hands of the creator. Something that I don't think anybody else in the stadium realized. They were too immersed in the game. I held my head in my hands and silently wept before I dared a peek. A peek that just then caught him looking down to his horror to see the cause of the pain. A large, sharp stone was embedded in his chest. He charged at his blue-faced enemy, but only fell back down in dizziness. His vision was blurring and his ability to speak was failing miserably. "Just like I drowned that Peel, number three, I think." The Rosian boasted as I could see Table's failing form; I let a few tears drop. Today, a wrongdoing man was going to leave Morg, and I dearly hoped he would be cared for. I watched on, horrified as the people around enjoyed the agony that was displayed. Then, the damp pillow of his grave shortly arose to meet him. Table would never see the end of the race. No, he would never find out who won. Life could vanish before you realized it was gone. For him, that's what had happened; he never realized he was dead until it was too late. The worst things in your life happen the same way. And the best way to cope is to accept what's happened and move on. But also don't forget to do better next time. Table, for example, made a grave mistake. He should've never doubted. That and the horrible crime that had all been because of a lie. The greatest gift wasn't mortal knowledge; it was life and knowing what comes after.

PART 2-THE FEAST

"I didn't win. I didn't win," I whispered in a panic. I found myself sitting at my own invention, a place to exchange food and words. And I just couldn't cope with the idea that I had lost. It was impossible to me; it just was. I was reeling at my surroundings and taking it all in with a gulp of fresh air. I was in a restaurant that was almost empty save for my table where I sat. It wasn't empty at all. Sitting across from me were three of the six racers, and one on my right, who had lost the game so far. Across from me and the one on the left was a long-haired, female Lox who I had heard was called Surely; in the middle was a Cor; and the one on the right was a muscular Peel. The Lox with her very human look, the Cor with his grey reflection and purple-ish, spiked hair, and the Peel who had a colourful assortment of paint on his ovalish appearance. Finally, there beside my own frame was the same Tralaxie I had tricked. The memory of throwing him out the train window still haunted my soul. It was true that I was selfish in having self-preservation in mind. But what would he say? Would he be disappointed? I searched it in his eyes and he comforted the thought.

"I really don't want to say it's alright. However, I think I will. I forgive you," he spoke with a curving smile and I was instantaneously lifted of most of the guilt I had been feeling. In this instant, he portrayed himself as caring and friendly. Lamp, one of my oldest friends, had been watching my performance and now I realized that his belief in there being a second life was most probably true. Even though the concept was lightly regarded in my culture, it was being pleasantly played out before my eyes. This was, I realize, too good to be true. And without a full table, a feast with future friends would never be a proper feast to the good times ahead. My left-hand side was empty and awaiting the last guest. But who would take it, the Rosian who undeniably won in the fight for life and possibly taking the game too seriously, or the Ancient. The Ancient who I had once heard was a carpenter back on his home world, earth. I examined the eyes of the three competitors who were engrossed in deep conversation. It looked to me like they were totally at home here, which wasn't surprising at all. They had already had time to adjust as they were erased from the game only minutes before I was.

"Welcome! I presume you were originally number seven?" the Cor began his introduction as the others listened with intent.

"I was, but you can call me Table."

"I will. I'm Darwin, and you probably know that I'm from Corinthia." I nodded to what the man in his thirties had to say. Darwin was posh and I could tell he was a perfectionist. The Cor then in turn went into a labelling of the other three at the table. "This is Bulwark. He's a wrestler, as you can see by his gigantic arms, and he's a Peel. That's Dropqa; she's a Tralaxie, and she's…

please remind me what you do!" I looked Bulwark over and could tell he was the most quiet and due to the appearance of strength, not very smart.

My thin eyebrows twitched as I learned of the Tralaxie's true gender. Then she spoke for herself. "I'm a ventriloquist, which is a rare occupation amongst my people. Yes, I have built a solid profession on an underrated art." She was timid, evidently had a sense of humor, and spoke in a sort-of whisper.

"Yes, and this here is...," Darwin was interrupted by the Lox.

"I can speak; I have a mouth, Darwin. My name is Surely. Since everybody is talking about their professions, I might as well blab away. I'm, or was, the owner of the universe's biggest coffee shop. I sold and archived every single type of coffee in the known worlds. This, I believe, is death. I'm dead, and this is the next world. I've always believed, so this is by far no surprise. But Darwin, he can't be a believer. You're not a believer. I mean you are a teacher on Corinthia, a teacher of atheism. But you just can't be," Surely introduced herself with zest in the way she spoke. I could tell she had a defensive and most likely feminist personality.

"As it happens, Surely, I am a believer. Or I try to be at least. Sometimes it's hard. The doubt keeps on coming, and never stops. But yes, I suppose I'm a believer. Actually, I have to be; my planet is a believing world. Everyone believes; they just do. They believe life has a purpose, has a reason to be, and has to end. We believe in a creator. Alas, we have to introduce ourselves in a waste of time before the last guest arrives. For this, my friend, is where we'll feast forever. Now speak on, before I capture your words."

"A feast; that sounds glorious! I'll be looking forward to that. Anyway, my name is Table. I'm a Morgian, and somehow responsible for this race. I know I'm not, not really. But it feels like it. Anyway, my profession, my work, is the fine art of food. I'm a chef and used to work for the biggest restaurant in the far and wide. I was fired 'cause one of my many dishes was found faulty by a customer. They made trouble for the owner of the expensive diner, and there was no choice for the owner but to let go of me. Ever since then, I've been on a quest. A quest for a book I'm writing on the greatest foods known to existence. And it's almost done," the short look into my life was interrupted by Bulwark as I got to the uncertain part. My book was in danger of incompletion.

"You won't be able to finish it, will you?" he sympathetically asked.

"I'll have to leave it behind; never finish the first actual piece of writing I've done."

"Maybe that's not true," Surely took over.

"We've been told by the only visible waitress that this place serves every single refreshment and nourishment known to all the corners of life. It's the perfect place to start again, Table," Dropqa encouraged.

I started, almost not believing what everyone said about this fantastical restaurant. It was really sounding better and better by the minute. "Is this real, Darwin?" I asked in disbelief.

"It is. No dreaming here. This is the real world, more real than what we've ever experienced!" Darwin confidently answered. Then the conversation ended as the other four guests talked about their lives, and the things they had left behind. Really I was part of the conversation, but I got distracted by the details that swarmed around. This restaurant had a sense of high class with its brightened atmosphere. And its many alcoves were set with beckoning tables, like the one we were sitting at. Our own light-wood table was laden with cutlery designed for each of our food-holding limbs. Most of us had two upper limbs, arms and hands, but the Peel had four instead of two. My observations also captured the thin, translucent covering that was underneath it all. It was meant to preserve the dining piece from mess. My sight zoomed out and I focused on the white booklet with a heading in my language. Glancing up, I noticed that the others were now reading their translated menus. I assumed that the rest had its own type of text according to the species and its language. This was the beauty of languages and names; it made each one of us unique. The art of variety. Which could only be done by immense power. I opened the booklet and my eyes popped figuratively out from their sockets. This was truly the feast. For each item I recognized, I was breath taken and my mouth watered by it. Even the unfamiliar looked delicious enough to eat the booklet. My taste buds were being tempted and soon the challenge arose on what I would order. This was interrupted, however, by the last guest who appeared by my side. It was the Rosian, and he had gotten the same fate as I did.

"Is this what I think it is?" he wore a look of guilt that would eventually fail to exist. Now he was the loud one, even though he wasn't saying much. I could tell by the way he quickly spoke and then nervously looked for a place to put his hands. He finally chose to awkwardly cross his arms, which meant to me that he was most likely not used to being socially close to anyone. I nodded at the question and then assured him that his act in the labyrinth had been justified.

"I don't think it matters anymore. What's your name, by the way? It's a bit of a starting tradition, telling our names and the things we've left behind," I explained to the last guest.

He hesitated, "Gefron. And before this happened, before the race happened, I was a neurosurgeon. One of the greatest neurosurgeons that existed in the realm of the medical sciences. Now, I don't know what I'll do."

"It's surreal, Gefron. But it's also, from what I've heard, glorious and fantastical. What number were you?"

"I started off as number three. Yeah, it is glorious and fantastic. But I don't understand how a loser can be rewarded. This is a reward of sorts, isn't it? If it is, this shouldn't be for us," Gefron sincerely sounded puzzled.

"No one's really a loser. Losers don't exist, Gefron. This is very much for us. Like who needs ultimate knowledge when you have access to all the foods of the universe? When I found myself here, I didn't believe what I saw. This wasn't at all what I thought losing would feel like. It's too good, I mumbled to myself as everyone up to you, slowly started to arrive," Darwin told about being the first guest in a raspy voice.

"I thought something very similar to that," Dropqa agreed, followed by Bulwark and Surely nodding their heads.

"I just got here, Gefron, and I'm stunned and amazed. I have a second chance at writing my food guide. I have found hope; I have found light." I said, ending our conversation as Bulwark reminded us of the food to come.

"Has everyone decided upon refreshments and their meal?" I looked at him and came to realize that a waitress was patiently standing at the end of the table. The silver colour of her skin and the emotionless eyes revealed that she was indeed mechanical. In her clutch was a grey, cylindrical device to go along with a yellow pad of paper. The few that hadn't made their minds up quickly decided and then told their wishes. She rapidly scrawled the orders onto the pad of paper and then it was my turn to order. I knew exactly what I wanted.

"I would like some Bubonic Plague for my refreshment and Cancer with a side-order of Malaria," I ordered. And as I said this, the thought of eventually getting this put before me, made me even hungrier. She scribbled my wanting down and then asked what size of glass I wanted the Bubonic Plague in. "A medium would be fine."

The waitress left and we continued our conversations. "Let me think; that would mean that…" I had pieced together the entire order and puzzle of the race. That evening, we had the feast of our dreams. And since then, we've been having one every day.

Transmission ended:

The ending behind 'The Feast,' worked with the idea about what if there was a species or group of species that could literally eat disease. We would be free from the most terrible and deadly illnesses out there. And in a way, each country, province, state, or continent could be considered a restaurant to these species. This part of the story was not intended to be offensive. So if it was, I apologize greatly.

—Anthony Unger

000002IIIIIIIII0000I0000I000002III000002IIIIIIIII:

NODDING OFF
BY AMBER UNGER

I opened my eyes to see an African-American staring at me with a stern expression. I had once again nodded off in Mrs. O'Brien's class.

"How *dare* you sleep in *my* class, young man?" She spoke with sass in her voice. Yet since I had gotten so used to her, it didn't make me feel as guilty as it once would've. I quickly sat up straight, sharply looking around. I noticed that we were already dismissed, for the class was completely empty. "As you have probably already noticed, you have been dismissed. But, since you were sleeping, you must first tell me what, is 13×12?" The answer almost immediately popped into my head. Grade 7 wasn't easy, but I had multiplication covered.

"The answer is 156, ma'am."

"Bravo! You may go now." For a moment, I thought she sounded a bit sarcastic. Though I also heard kindness, and I think she was a little impressed. I swiftly packed my backpack, slung it over my shoulder, and I began on my way home. Once there, I went to my room and neatly placed my backpack in a corner. I then walked back down the hallway to the kitchen, expecting my mom to be there. Of course, she was.

"Hey, Mom, I'm finally home!"

"What took you so long, hanging out with your girlfriend?" she teased me playfully.

"Mom!" I groaned.

She chuckled. "I was just kidding!"

"Oh, I know *that*! It's just… Well, oh, I don't know. I guess I just don't like it when you tease me about having a girlfriend," I explained, my voice suddenly becoming serious.

"Whether you like being teased or not, you still have to go wash your hands before eating supper."

"Alright, I suppose I can't resist your cheese-covered rice patties."

"Why, thank you! Now chop, chop!" I was sure she had just made a terrible pun, but she could be unpredictable sometimes. Racing past the kitchen table and through a doorway to the living space, I reached the bathroom door, and skidded to a stop. Click! The door opened wide, waiting for me to enter its gaping mouth. I quickly washed my hands, almost forgetting the soap. Then I bolted out of the bathroom, and back into the kitchen. "You really are full of energy, aren't you?"

“He he! I am, am I?”

“Well, you *are* running through the hall although I’m always telling you to slow down a bit.”

“Okay, okay. So I’m full of energy. Does it *really* matter that much?”

“If you’re going to be knocking down chairs and furniture, then yes, it does.” We ended the conversation there. The food *was* getting cold, after all. Once we had eaten a delicious meal of cheese-covered rice patties and some leftover egg salad sandwiches, we each went to our separate bedrooms. As I settled down in my bed, I thought about just how dull my day-to-day life was. This very thought made me more than excited for tomorrow morning.

The next morning, I woke up full of energy and ready to start the day. I quickly got dressed, went to the kitchen, and made myself some cereal, which I scarfed down like a mad man. It was ‘Kellogg’s Jif’ cereal, my third favorite. “Bye, Mom. I’m going now!” I yelled cheerfully.

“Wha…?” her sleepy voice rang in my ears as I ran out the open door and toward the park. The park was down my street, on the left, and then once to the right. Finally, I took a left, and there it was with its baseball diamond, two play structures, and a soccer field. Not to mention a deep forest beyond the park. There, waiting for me were my friends, Andrew and Phillip.

“Hey, Benjamin! What took you so long? It’s already 8:30.”

“Oh, hi, Andrew! I woke up a bit late today.”

“So, what are we waiting for? Let’s go!”

“Do you always have to be so impatient, Phillip?” Andrew snapped a little too harshly.

"Calm down, boys!" We all laughed at my natural comedy.

"You just love saving the moment, don't you?" Andrew remarked.

"Maybe I don't, maybe I do." The moment ended in more laughter, and we ran off into the distance. Farther off into the park, past the play structure, and into the forest. We were searching for adventure, for something to live for. When we got to the brink of the forest, excited whispers were exchanged. This was where our real adventure began.

"It's finally time," Phillip announced excitedly while adjusting his brand new pair of glasses.

"After months of planning, we're here. Ready to change our lives," said the over-enthusiastic Andrew.

"Um, don't you think you exaggerated just a *little bit* too much?" I argued.

"Nah," he replied as he swatted the air.

"Well, suit yourself." We moved forward and soon came to a clearing.

"Wow! This really is majestic," I said in awe.

"It is, isn't it?" an unfamiliar voice came from behind us.

We turned around to follow the sound.

"Who are you?" It was Andrew who asked the question, and there was some fear in his voice as he tried to uncover the identity of the person who was no longer there.

"Huh? Where'd they go?" Phillip was the most perplexed of us all.

We all stood there, our mouths ajar, wondering what to do next. We spun around, and the next thing we knew was that surprisingly there, in front of us, was the mysterious voice we had heard. It definitely wasn't what we were expecting, but there it was. A bear-like being was partially blocking the path that led forward. It was also waiting for Andrew to say something. He was, after all, kind of the leader of our little group. I decided to speak up before Andrew messed anything up, only nothing really came out.

"I - um - we," was all that left my lips.

"I understand. You humans often get nervous when meeting new creatures," her voice was soft, like that of a mother's.

"So, are you going to tell me your names, or should I not be asking that??

"No, it's just that we wanted to know *your* name first," Andrew said.

Phillip and I both cast Andrew a confused and annoyed glance.

He merely shrugged and mouthed, "So what?"

I rolled my eyes at him. The creature spoke again, abruptly cutting off any more words from Phillip or me.

"Well, if you're so eager to know, my name is Klashimba."

"Nice to meet you. I'm Andrew. And this is Phillip and Benjamin," he motioned toward us.

"Hello, Benjamin, Phillip, and Andrew. I hear that you boys are looking for adventure?"

"Wait, how do you know that?" Phillip asked, worry creeping into his voice.

"I have my ways," she replied hastily. "So, with that aside, I have something to show you."

"Wait, wait, wait; you expect us to just trust you? Just like that?" I protested.

"Hey, you're the ones who want adventure," Klashimba answered.

"She's got a point," Phillip said.

"Yeah," I agreed.

"Therefore, we will come with you. Reluctantly," Andrew concluded.

Klashimba led the little troop through a thorny, eerie, and narrow trail to a huge rock with a wooden door built into it.

"Shall we enter?"

"I suppose so," Andrew stole the words directly from my mouth. I was mildly frustrated with the detail and I almost felt like taking my wrath upon him, but I fully dismissed it. Shaking out of my thoughts, I returned to the scene. We were already within the holding of the boulder and Klashimba was asking if anyone was thirsty. It was a cozy dwelling with very few articles of furniture due to the size of the boulder. An assortment of gray, cushioned chairs sat in lonely serenity around a dark brown table. Not being thirsty, Phillip and Andrew declined the offer. As soon as Klashimba got to me, I started scanning the furniture. It seemed eccentric and advanced as if it was from another planet, or time.

"Uh, Ben, aren't you going to answer me?"

"Huh? What? Yeah?"

"I asked if you wanted something," she repeated patiently.

"Oh! Hmm… I'll just have a glass of water, please."

"Nothing to eat?"

"No, I'm fine, really."

"Alright," she said and pranced off with a slight hop, probably meaning she was filled with glee knowing at least someone had accepted her offer. After a few seconds, she was back and firmly gripping something in her hand that did not look like water.

"Um, what's this?" I asked nervously, thinking this would end horribly.

"It's something I call [4]Jemblaredo. It is a mix of pecans, berries, orange peel, sticks, dark chocolate, pickles, lemon juice, leaves, and a pinch of salt for extra flavor. Wait, I can't forget the Dorito on top. By the way, it's supposed to be a garnish. The Dorito, I mean."

It didn't look tasty. It didn't sound tasty. And it certainly didn't taste like a tasty thing would. I had taken a sip, and I absolutely regretted it.

"It's good," I swallowed, struggling to smile. It tasted sour, but there were other unmentionable tastes that really brought the drink together. She seemed to not notice that I was lying. But she did notice my friends' nervous faces.

Klashimba sighed, "If you don't want to try it, then go ahead and avoid it. I have no interest in forcing anybody to do anything they don't want to." She left the small room by way of a doorway found on the left side of the room.

"I'm just gonna go wash my hands." As soon as she left us alone in the living room, we concluded that maybe, just maybe, it wasn't a good idea to trust Klashimba after all. So we started planning our escape.

"We'll leave the boulder when she isn't looking and run until we leave her behind. Then we'll continue our adventure," I explained in a hushed tone, also not realizing that we could already escape at any moment.

---

4 Pronounced Jem-blah-ray-doo

“Wait, what if we get lost?” Phillip asked in fear.

“I’m sure we’ll figure something out,” I assured him.

“Everything will be perfectly according to plan. You really don’t need to worry,” Andrew added, being his usual over-confident self.

“Shh… Klashimba’s coming!” warned Phillip.

We acted casually as she entered the living space, and she didn’t suspect us planning anything against her at all. Sneakily inching toward the door, we noticed Klashimba had once again left the room. We dashed out the entrance to find ourselves in a strange area. It was nothing at all like where we were originally. For when we looked around, there were barely any trees. I also noticed that we were standing on a rocky hill. And in the distance, there were several sheep spread across the land. Even though we were afraid of getting lost, we briskly headed toward the horizon in fear of Klashimba catching up to us. Soon after, we found ourselves leaning against a quaint building, panting with exhaustion. It was a shack made of logs, which made it more of a cabin in the middle of a flat nowhere. To the right hand side of the only visible door was a large, black, wooden sign with white-carved words. On the other side of the door, was a tall, four-framed window. Being the active youngins we were, we didn’t bother reading the sign, but caught the word, ‘store’. Once we were partially recovered, we gazed around us at the trees that now dotted the green grass, detailing it a bit more. And then after fully recovering, we entered the store. Inside, an aged man stood behind a counter, waiting for us. Not fully noting any of the organized details of a general-store, we stepped closer to the counter.

"G'day! How may I help you?" the old man spoke with a soft, thick, Scottish accent.

"We would like to know where we are," I replied confidently.

"Well, you're in Glensburg, of course. Where did ya think you were?" He rolled his r's naturally, as if he'd been doing it since he was a toddler.

"Um, we actually had no idea where we were, really. By the way, where exactly *is* Glensburg?" I tried to roll my r's like he did, but failed miserably.

"Don'tcha know that we're in Scotland, laddie?"

"No, I… I mean… we, didn't know that," I faltered.

"If that's it, then I'd be going off on me tea break now," he stood up from a stool behind the counter. The counter was tall, so you couldn't tell if he had a kilt or not. But I imagined him with a black, grey, and gray-blue kilt.

"Yes, that's it. Have a good tea break!"

"And you have a good day!" he uttered before stepping through an open door closed behind him.

As we left to continue our journey through Scotland, Phillip pointed out, "I've always wanted to go to Scotland."

The silence that followed afterwards was quite awkward. We kept travelling like no one ever said anything. I felt at ease now, and very peaceful although I wasn't sure how this day could get any worse or if it could even get better. Suddenly, we heard something from behind us, footsteps and the promise of someone or something creeping up. Fearing the worst, we turned around and saw to our disappointment that it was Klashimba. We instantly started running. Only a few steps in, we found ourselves face to face with Klashimba.

"So," she began.

"Are you going to apologize for tricking us here because your apology is not accepted," Andrew hastily interrupted.

"Andrew!" I whispered through gritted teeth and with eyes directed at him.

"No, really, it's what I deserve. I mean, I did bring you here. But not intentionally. In fact, that's not at all what I came here to tell you."

"Then what *did* you come to tell us?" It was now Phillip who spoke up.

"Okay. I have been meaning to tell you. The boulder that I led you into, is, let's say, alive. It moves around, and even migrates. When I met you in the forest, I hoped that if I showed the three of you this, you'd want to somehow help me convince the boulder to let me live in it. That's why I brought you to my boulder in the first place. You were, after all, looking for adventure."

"But how would we communicate with it?" Phillip asked.

"That's exactly the problem. I need to find a way to talk to it so that I can continue living the peaceful life I used to live, except a little more peacefully."

"Hmm. We understand your dilemma now, but why don't you just move somewhere else?" I solemnly inquired.

"You see, it's the cheapest I can afford. And it was the only place resembling anything to a cave that I could find," Klashimba explained.

"And why didn't you tell us sooner?" Andrew added.

"I mean, I was first going to give you refreshments, and then tell you everything, but you left too soon," Klashimba replied.

"Then, you've found the perfect team!" I exclaimed.

After another detailed discussion about it, we set to work finding different strategies of communicating with the oversized rock. While we were doing this, we were also heading off to where we would use these strategies. Then, once at the boulder, Klashimba realized we were right. It wasn't communicating that we had to figure out, but where to look for a new home and then moving out. So, we started thinking of places where Klashimba could possibly live. And in the end, we eventually thought of something that might work.

"Hey! I think I recall seeing a cave on our way here," Phillip threw out the idea.

Surprised, I replied, "Really? You've got to show us!"

"The thing is, I meant here as in, to the forest. Back in Gytrel, home."

"*What*?!" Andrew stood up, astonished. "Back home?!"

"Yeah," Phillip returned.

"I guess it *is* our only chance of finding Klashimba a home. Besides, at least we'll be able to see her more often," I added hopefully. I was just now starting to warm up to her.

"True," Andrew had calmed down a bit, now seeing the privileges in our plan.

"Now," Klashimba finally spoke up, "we have to find a way to get back home."

"You know what? We thought we were wrong, but we weren't. We *do* have to try to speak with the rock. We're going to ask it to help us back to Gytrel," I said, trying to sound heroic and wise.

“Solid plan, Ben. Only, what if we *can’t* communicate with it?” Andrew protested.

“Let’s not get ahead of ourselves *just* yet,” I advised as we all stood at the very entrance of the boulder.

“How shall we start?” Klashimba asked.

“By brainstorming,” Phillip suggested brightly.

“So, basically, you want us to write all of our ideas on a piece of paper and try all of them on the massive stone,” said Klashimba.

“Yep!” Andrew, Phillip, and I simultaneously agreed.

“Well, if you say so.” We sprang through the door of the boulder and found our supplies. We then sat down on the nearest chairs that lined Klashimba’s only table, and began jotting down ideas. I had four on my page, and I assumed the others each had about seven. Later, when we had every single idea in mind placed on our papers, we wandered out the door to put it in action. Our first attempt went well, although it didn’t fully work. The attempt was an assortment of dance moves that Klashimba learned over the years from her bear and human hybrids. They were apparently to her, her species’ version of sign language. After more attempts, it was our very last idea that truly worked. We expressed our plight the way we would talk to each other, by speaking English. “Salutations,” Klashimba kindly greeted him.

“Hello,” he said in a faint, unsatisfied, New Yorkan.

“We have come to ask you for a favor. And um… I don’t want to sound rude, or anything. But if you’d be willing to transport us back to where you originally picked us up, that would be more than fantastic!”

"For one price," the boulder surprised Klashimba with a straight answer that wasn't "No! Now leave me alone!"

"Say, wha-at?!" Klashimba had really expected the answer "no." Like when you ask your parents for something you know they'll never get you, but they do.

"You have to either find me or help me find a girlfriend."

"Are you sure that's what you want? There's *nothing* else you want? Nothing?" Klashimba asked.

"I am as sure as I'll ever be," he confirmed.

"If so, then deal," we all said in unison after we had discussed it in a huddle.

"Since this quest is for me, may I suggest Easter Island? There will be plenty of ladies there, I'm sure of it." I imagined the rock winking as he said that, though he had no face.

"What! Never! There's no one there except a bunch'a rocks. *I* think, yes *I* think, we should go to the Swiss Alps. There's even more rocks there *and*, it's a mountain range!" I interjected another idea into the conversation.

"First of all, we're *looking* for a bunch of rocks, and second of all, Easter Island is a *brilliant* idea," Andrew defended the grey, rocky, and not very round ball.

"Easter Island, it is!" Phillip finalized.

"Get in and let the adventure begin!" the rock shouted enthusiastically. "Oh, and, if you would like to know, my name is Hiyay." Once he had finished speaking, we re-entered the rock and sat down at the ornate chairs once again and waited. There was nothing to wait for though. We poked each of our heads outside to find that we were not on Easter Island, but on a beach in mere seconds. "Sorry.

Bit of a detour there. Nothing to worry about; it's all fine. I just stopped to rest since it's getting dark. Good night!"

"We understand perfectly other than the fact that it's only... zzz...," I was too tired to protest anymore as I fell to the rugged floor of the boulder.

"Good night," Klashimba, Phillip, and Andrew simultaneously entreated. I didn't wish anyone a good night because I was, as you know, asleep.

The next morning, I woke up to the sound of my friends getting ready. "What time is it?" I asked drowsily.

"It's 8:03. Get ready!" Andrew informed as well as commanded me.

"Okay," I closed my eyes for five more seconds and then got up to get dressed. Once I had remembered that we actually didn't have any fresh clothes with us, I headed over to the table, full with supplies, and took what I needed. "What are these for?" I asked.

"For our journey to Easter Island, of course!" Andrew put his forehead on his outstretched palm and then lifted it, leaving it floating in the air.

"But why would we need *climbing* equipment?" I questioned, not getting the full picture.

"Well, maybe there would be a *lovely* rock on top of one of those head things," Andrew rolled his eyes while making two peace signs which he folded and unfolded continuously during the word lovely.

"Is everybody ready to take a trip to Easter Island where everything. is fun and sun?" Klashimba described the isle the way an advertiser would talk about a vacation spot.

"Mmm hmm!" Phillip mumbled excitedly.

"Oh yeah!" Andrew shouted with enthusiasm as he leapt.

"Ready as I'll ever be!" I ended the chain of excitement.

"Then, let's be off! Hiyay, to the island where Easter is always a thing!" Klashimba pointed her index finger toward the boulder's only exit. With that, the rest of us turned to do so also.

Before we could make it completely outside, Hiyay broke out the terrible truth, "We've been here for over ten minutes," using a monotonous tone of voice. The plainness of his voice sank deep into my soul.

We carried on. The sights of the area were quite pleasing. 'Oohs' and 'aahs' were shared throughout the time we were there.

"Ughh! How long does it *take* just to spot some cute rock?" Andrew moaned wearily with sarcasm mixed into a few of the words.

We continued to search until we all felt too exhausted to stand any longer.

Just then, the boulder cried out, "There she is!"

"I'm sorry, but who?" I questioned.

"The most attractive woman I have ever seen." And there she was, peeking out shyly from behind a moai head, which was on top of a high and grassy cliff. It was a stone statue of a face along with its never ending line of look-alikes. The high and grassy cliff looked out toward the vast, blue, and green ocean. Not too far in the distance, I could see a puny grey and brown blob that looked a lot like another island. A *big* island. But that's beside the matter. We walked slowly up the cliff, cautiously eyeing the sharp edges that threatened to trip us and throw us off down the cliff. We finally got to the top and brought the medium, although heavy rock back with us to Klashimba's former home. While they got to know each other better, Klashimba, Andrew, Phillip and I explored a little longer. I showed everyone the island I found and the answer I received was shocking.

"It's great that you found that island, Ben, because we might need it," I was truly abashed.

"Huh? Why would we need some random island?" I queried.

"While all of you were fetching Hiyay's new friend, I went back down ahead of you and had a little chat with him. He said that he has grown too weary to transport you all the way to your hometown, but he should still have enough energy to teleport us to the island you just pointed to. From there, we *should* be able to find a way back to Gytrel. *And*, we'll most likely be closer that way," Klashimba broke the news in her most uplifting voice.

"You know what, that's actually a pretty good idea!" I put in cheerily.

"I don't know," Phillip added with uncertainty.

"Yeah, well, I think you're just being optimistic," Andrew argued.

"I know you two don't really agree with it, but it's our best choice," Klashimba concluded. So that's what we did. After arriving on the island, we asked some of the locals if they knew how we could get back to Gytrel. They mentioned that the island had an airport. We received directions and then headed toward the airport. The next thing we knew—we were home. Klashimba found the cave that Phillip had mentioned, and Andrew, Phillip and I all dragged ourselves back to our houses. Phillip had finally arrived home and was ready to relax, but as soon as he plopped down on the couch, his mother and father came bursting through the door. They were so overwhelmed with joy that they ended up hugging him. When he got to his house, Andrew got a little surprise.

"Andrew! You're finally back!" his mom exclaimed once he had shut the door. "Guess what?"

"What?" Andrew asked nervously.

"We're going to Scotland!" Andrew's jaw dropped open.

My ending, however, was different. As soon as I got home, I ran straight to bed and nodded off to sleep. I had realized that adventure wasn't what it really seemed.

000000IIIII200000IIIII200000000:

ARTHUR

"The string of words,
'I am the child of the cube, never left me.'"

They haunt me as I transition from that dark place to life after. They keep me thinking, my mouth never moving but my mind is at work. That nightmare with the walls and waking up imprisoned has left me in ruins but also has given me a piece of my identity back. I remember now why I am the way I am. I know how I got into the hospital in the first place, and it ain't a cheerful memory. However in the end, I've eventually been set free. But I'm not, no matter how hard I try. My past keeps me down, making it so difficult to get back up again. I am chained to my nightmares and realities. "Here I am, several weeks after waking up from my mental coma. I'm on the roof of the hospital. I still find myself in disbelief that I'm free; it's been so long." Not knowing if it was a good thing I was released or not, I ask myself "could I harm another human being? And if not, could I ever harm a cute, cuddly creature like a grey, fluffball of a bunny?" I could be dangerous and not know it. Alas though, I don't think I can be. I'm not in the cube but I'll always be reminded that the cube had an eternal hold on my very being. I will always be the child in my mind, as he kicks and hits the walls imprisoning him. 'Let me out! Let me out!' I scream, but no one hears me. Are we all children, I don't know? All I know is that I'm the child of the cube. And I'm glad no one's behind me listening. If they did, they would think that I'm not truly better. It's my mind, it's overflowing. And due to this, I talk to myself. "They would lock me up again, treat me like the ill man I was." My mind is still fragile from all that's happened, and that means nothing is quite real. "My thinking is the only thing keeping me sane," I tell myself as the cold wind of autumn blows over my face. It comforts me like the gentle touch of a mother's fingers. The only mother I have is nature. "To the only knowledge I know of my mother is that she left me when I was young. I can assume she did so after my father died. I was too much of a responsibility and I reminded her of him."

I can still hear that fateful sentence, "Pack your bags. You're going for a visit, Arthur."

"Where am I going, Mommy?" I had used that same exact combination of words. She told me it was a surprise, and we got into our family four-seater, and were off down the quiet, dark street. The vehicle parked right next to the city's orphanage, and my mother led me to the door with two suitcases of toys and clothes. She rang the doorbell and was off as tears formed in my eyes. I cried for her as rain poured down on my hatted head. She left me cold, and afraid, at a place where everyone who didn't have a home was their own home. The time at Grim's orphanage was a part of the fall I would experience where nothing felt like it should. Grim was a tall, skinny man, wearing a mask of white, and I dreaded him for he was harsh and mistreated the ones he said he cared for. He said he loved them in a fatherly way but he called them trash and bullied them like they were exactly that. This broke my heart even further and I knew my life would be a rollercoaster of shades clashing together to form a cloud of misery. All that emotion and grief translated into a profession when I was in middle school. I wanted to be a painter. A little bit like the greatest there was, and a lot like myself. I wanted my paintings to take flight on the canvas. A flick of a brush like the flick of a wand, it was all magic to me. It was in the time when I was in middle school that I had the biggest problem of being bullied. That never ended. It created a rotten hole where happiness should've been and it transformed me into a monster. Above me a whooshing flight catches me off guard as a claw grabs me by the throat and I am thrown across the roof. Not being able to stop the greeting tarmac under my rear end I sat startled and in dismay. Dismay, for perhaps I wasn't ready to be released yet. A tunnel of colours flashed before me in the blue, Canadian sky. Then, the claw and the toss to the tarmac repeated itself again and again. It was gone as any recollection of it faded to the depths of the cube.

I clutch my head in an attempt to get rid of the rainbow tunnel. "Get it out, get it out!" I pull myself up the chimney wall, directly beside the only door downstairs. My curly frock of brown jiggled, "I must have somehow bumped against its thin, metal surface. For I can hear it," I pause to listen. "Someone is coming up the stairs."

Rushing from the door to the edge again, I pretend the claw never happened. "Leave me alone, claw!"

I look to the sky where it originated not too long ago. I don't want them to take me again. I'm fine… I'm fine! I am mentally fine!"

The fire door opens but I stay where I am, gazing down at Quebec with its little houses in neat rows.

"Houses here, and there, a bridge in the far right, and people. Oh so many people going their, oh, so many ways."

"It is like that, isn't it?" a feminine voice made me turn around to face her.

"Hello, Andrea!" I politely grace her as she drops a pair of folding chairs to the tarmac. Setting up a plastic, white, folding table she took the chairs and set them up on either end. In her other hand, she carried a tall thermos, which she gave to me to hold.

"Isn't it chilly out here?" is all she says.

Setting up a plastic, white, folding table she took the chairs and set them up on either end.

"I like it."

"I suppose you do! Did I by any chance hear you talking to yourself? Because you know, if you did, we would have to treat you again, wouldn't we?" Andrea smiled mischievously. She drew a checkered table spread from her nurse outfit.

I felt frightened for that one moment, and she must've seen it, because she reacted with a laugh. "Only kidding! That's normal you know. It means we're lonely when we do that. We speak to the heavens when we do," the nurse took my hand, and folding the rim of her aqua-blue skirt, sits down. I sit down as well.

"I guess it does," I chuckled with reassurance. Then glancing down at the thermos, I give it back. "Coffee?"

"Afraid not, and I know how much you love the bitter poison, but we must settle on the sweet poison instead. They were out in the kitchen," uncapping the thermos, she filled the cap back. "I'm afraid I've also forgotten cups. So I'll just have to swig it like a bottle of the finest wine, but with less posh precision," she smiled again with a twinkle in her blue eyes. I graciously took the cap of hot chocolate she offered to me, and then took a careful sip.

"I know you were talking to yourself, Arthur!" Andrea took a sip, burning her lip, and cursing it off. "Aah hot!"

"What can I say to make you believe I wasn't," the nurse sternly looked at him. "Oh you're right, I was. I just need somebody to talk to I guess." I take a sip as she copies my action.

"It's a good thing I thought of joining you up here. I have always been there for you know," she moved her plastic chair closer. "What were you talking about? I could be the one to listen, hear what you have to say."

I frowned as I finished the chocolate and put the cap down on the table, "It was about my past. I was trying to make sense. Of it all. The confusion and all the horrible things. I don't think you would like it."

"Of course I would. I would love it. I mean it's all horrible, but I will grieve for you, Arthur. I care about you." Taking the cap, she refilled it. "Where were we? I believe you were telling me of your bullying issue when you were young. You said it made you miserable. Like when your blood mother left you at Greven's orphanage."

The memories came flooding back, "My love for art," I mumbled as I took the cap and quietly sipped away.

"You should show me some of your art," she said. She looked and sounded interested.

"I burnt all, Andrea! It caused me pain, to know that he's still out there."

Now, her brows peaked and she leaned over the table, "Who, Arthur? Who's still out there? And why did he cause you pain?" Making herself comfortable, she sat back and listened.

I wanted to ask her why I should tell her anything, why she cared. But I knew. Over the time I had been subjected here at the hospital, she had grown fond of me. And I, I felt something. I didn't know what it felt like to have a relationship with another human being. Not anymore, that is.

Downing the cap, I began. "The day I was left, the time in the orphanage. I found peace in art and the things I created. The moment my eyes saw a painting, art, I fell in love."

"May I interrupt?" an intermissive question was politely said as she took a sip, not wanting to miss a detail. I nodded as I continued again.

"'A Sunday Afternoon on the Island of Grande La Jatte'. Georges Seurat's finest piece. The colour and lines fascinated me; they told a story of beauty and a perfect world." Hesitating on what I was going to say, I recollected the fading memories of the claw. It wasn't real, just my imagination. And so this could be a dream as well.

"Beautiful painting if I might add. Are you alright?" she asked, sounding was worried.

"I'm fine. Are you a painter yourself?" I changed the topic.

"Yes, I am. I run a small studio in my flat. And I sell prints. You should come sometime, show me your art skills. For now, however, on with your story," my one-person audience intently listened.

"The year was 1971 and I was twenty-eight. I was in college at the time and I met an angel that never ceased to amaze me. She had a lock of chestnut brown that covered a head that could never be bald. What a thought, my angel with a bald head!"

"What was her name?" Andrea interrupted again.

"I'll get to it; hold your horses! I loved her; she loved me. And one day, we had a picnic. It was in July and a beautiful day was upon us. Andrea suggested…." It couldn't be… their names were the same.

"Oh, she has the same name, Arthur. Why haven't you told me this before?"

"I don't… I don't know why I didn't see it before. But it can't be…," I said with disbelief as I played the name over and over in my head. *Andrea, Andrea.* "But to the point, she suggested that we take a walk through the forest beside the college, and I knew she had something up her sleeve. You see, my Andrea had always been a keen admirer of plans. She was precise, knew exactly how the day was to be, even though nothing ever goes to plan. That day certainly didn't go as planned. For later on that day, I found out that she really did have something up her sleeves. We walked and talked as she wanted, always keeping on the path, and never straying from casual talk. It was noon and we decided to have that picnic that she had prepared for. So we sat down on the dirt path and unwrapped the large basket she had brought along. I helped her with laying everything out on the checkered cloth…," I paused. The checkered cloth. Now this was indeed one too many, the same name, and now the same cloth. Were these coincidences, or connections? I pushed the observation aside while the present Andrea didn't take notice. "It was a sight I will never forget. The picnic blanket was covered with an assortment of everything from pizza to foreign foods that she had said had been an enjoyment to create from a recipe. In my opinion, it didn't matter what it was as long as it was edible and had something of a good appearance to it. We ate, laughed at the jokes that would seem lame to anybody else, and talked about her job at the local 'Renaud-Bray'. Of course, 'Renaud-Bray' being the largest line of bookstores here. And speaking about locale, Andrea was also studying at the same college as I, but drama, and not art.

"'It's going well,' she had said in a strong voice. 'Today alone, I sold twice as many Shakespearian works than I normally do.' Interesting, I thought July was a month of going to the beach, eating ice cream, and going to the theaters, not reading Shakespeare. Andrea retorted to what I had said about Shakespeare. 'Silly, the art of play acting is for anytime.' Those words echo in my mind. They remind me that that day things didn't go as planned at all."

I take a long-needed break as I give the nurse my cap, and she in turn shook the thermos, almost empty now. Dividing the rest of the hot chocolate between the two of us, I took the cap and had my last sips. She in turn drank the thermos' last drops a little slower.

"Go on, Arthur!" she pleaded of me.

"We finished the picnic and said our goodbyes before setting a meeting point for the next day. Come to think of it, I wonder why she didn't give me the ring at the picnic."

"Maybe she was afraid you would say no!" the nurse brought out his inner fear about the situation.

"Perhaps that is so, Andrea. We packed away the rest of the food, and went our separate ways. I headed back the way we had come and she headed further into the forest. That brush of forest was a passageway from one part of the college, to the other. Except her way was the long way. She was out of sight and I was heading for campus… when I heard that awful pitch rising into the air. It broke the silence that had been left by our conversation. I changed the direction of my walk and ran till my breath was dying in my throat. I turned the corner where she had gone through, and where the woods started breaking into the other side of the campus. But I couldn't go any further. Because there she was, the life drained out in mere minutes. My eyes teared up and my hand comforted the gasp that was uttered. This couldn't be real. It couldn't be real and for the longest time I struggled with the reality of what had happened. Was it all a nightmare, a fake reality?"

I paused, looking thoughtfully into present Andrea's eyes. "I told myself, no, it wasn't. And even though I said this to myself I knew the truth, and it ripped me apart. At the time, there was a flutter of movement somewhere close by, but I was too wrapped up in what happened to do anything about it. I went to her side and tugged on her lifeless body, not wanting it to be true. 'My Andrea, don't be dead! Don't be. Please don't,' more tears and finally something happened that made the turn of events even worse. A little green box fell out of her pocket. That was how I discovered the ring. Shuddering at the thought that she was going to ask an important question, one that would change my life, I opened it. I was filled with anger, emotion just boiling over. What in the world could do such a thing to an innocent soul? It was a monster who had done this, not anything like you or me."

Nurse Andrea nodded, "There's a monster in all of us. One we have to never let out and control us."

I continued, feeling the cold breath of the wind fiercer than ever.

"Finally seeing the crimson marks on the ground, I put it together with what appeared to be a wooden point beside it. The weapon. It had broken off from something, but what? I went over it in my head, still telling myself it wasn't, couldn't be happening. After that rushed semester, I left the college and tried living my life. I tried forgetting the pain by doing what I loved. I moved to a rural part of the city, and got a low-paying job as an apprentice to a local artist. It wasn't much but an inheritance from my father in the bank and a stash of savings, that also helped me through. After years of living this new life, doing what I did best, and keeping a lot to myself, it all came back. I was finally getting over the bad memory in the forest when I made a discovery. One that ruined everything for me as it once had. It was an ordinary day, waking up in my rented bungalow and driving to work with an old rust bucket truck. The drive to my employer's flat in Quebec city was long, but I got there in half an hour's time. Working for [5]Truci meant that he taught me how to become better at putting paint to canvas. It also meant he paid me each day for being the only employee in his art shop. This entailed selling prints, assisting customers find what they wanted, and giving out cheap tutorials. Once the day was done, I stopped by his empty office to drop off the earnings. And looking back to that day I realize I didn't at all know whom I worked for. Truci wasn't who I thought he was. He was concealing something that I should've never found. To one side of the office, the man had a roll top desk that he frequently used to jot notes and entries into his journal. Having secretly seen him reveal a hidden compartment under one of the desk drawers, I pulled the even-more-hidden latch on the drawer. It was located on the inside corner of the drawer door, and could easily be missed. Before doing so, I called out for the professional artist

5 True-chee

to make absolute sure I wouldn't be caught red-handed. He wasn't there, and I assumed he had popped out for something. Opening the hidden compartment, I locked sights with a tattered, peeling book. No words were on the cover, just a blank white space. Opening it, I flicked through, curious as to what the man constantly wrote. Was he secretly an addicted novelist, someone who loved to write but was embarrassed to share it with others? Or was it something even more horrible? It was while I flicked through the journal's pages that I fell upon an entry. That's all the book was, entries and sometimes photographs of what I could only see as memories of growing up. I took in the date at the top left, and it brought that despair back. It was the same day my Andrea had left my side." A pigeon passed by as I shifted in the chair.

"I was filled with a sinking anxiety of what I would read next. But I risked everything I had rebuilt to take away those emotions I had felt. Maybe, just maybe, this had been meant for me to find. So I read on. And as I read the entry I was overfilled with emotions I simply couldn't keep in any more. Anger, sadness, hopelessness, and fear. They spun around as I read the description of what happened that day. He was, at the time, a cook for the college cafeteria. He wrote it as being under-appreciated. Truci had despised the job but he knew that he didn't have much choice. It was this or unemployment. He would have to search and search for something different. It was the same day that we had that picnic, when he had gotten fired. He flew out of the main entrance to the college, enraged, fists balled up. He had tried so very hard. And even though part of him wouldn't miss it, he was at a loss as to what to do next. Having his spare paintbrush with him like he always did, he always brought at least one along in case the time arose when he'd need it. He sharpened them under a tree. Putting away his pen knife, he made his way to the parking lot, but stopped by the forest entryway. He could hear talking, laughter, and then with hate for everything to do with the college, he sat back down under the tree. Taking out his journal, he wrote until he saw the tall figure of his used-to-be boss. Standing up, he kept his anger as concealed as possible as he was greeted with sympathy. The principal had talked to him about how he was sorry it had to go like this, that they had no choice."

"We're considering someone who has more experience and desire to work!" Truci had written down in his journal.

"The principal left him, informing him that he had to leave immediately, or the police would be called. After that, he told about how his anger took control of him so much that he tightly gripped the sharpened paintbrush and that's when the mistake happened. That's all he said, over and over: 'I made a mistake… made a mistake.' I couldn't read any more after that. I shut it closed, threw it back into the compartment and closed it, and the drawer. I had found the one responsible for dear Andrea's death. And I could tell it had damaged both the professional painter and me. My respect for him and his work had, must I say, certainly been dented. Stopping in my trails, I had failed to hear the shop door opening as Truci came back. Standing in the doorway to his office, the owner with his white-streaked hair went to the roll top and dropped a bulging grocery bag on it."

"We were empty of canvas and I brought some Chinese. Gladly stay for supper!" he said as he emptied the bag while I clenched my fists. Scanning the office, I saw an easel in the corner that I had never seen before. In fact, I had never been in his office in the first place; otherwise, I would've seen it. On the easel's tray was a row of brushes and three paint bottles. But the thing that backed up my newfound discovery was that the wooden end of each brush was sharpened to a point. I swiftly took one, and then stood there behind him with indecision. A part of me wanted him to die for what he did. But also, another part was telling me that I would be just as bad as him. I would be just as much of a monster as he was. The rest is muddled but I distinctly remember asking him why. Then, a conversation ensued where he asked what I was talking about. "You know. Your journal and Andrea." He hesitantly showed an expression of regret. "That was the worst mistake I have ever made. It was a silly thing to get mad over, but I couldn't control myself as pure rage took me over. But wait, how do you know?" Before I could move the brush aside, he turned his body and walked right into the awaiting paintbrush. Blind rage was a curse and now I was the bearer of it. Even though it was more of an accident than what had happened to Andrea, I still had anger in my heart. We stared at each other, both speechless as he grabbed the brush and used my shoulder as support. The stomach wound was already turning bright-crimson as his face went pale." "'You were there that day, weren't you?' he asked me."

"I aided the dying painter to the shop floor. 'I was, yes! I'm sorry. So sorry. I didn't mean to. I didn't!'"

I was shaking as I apologized, but he shook his head and assured me that it was inevitable. He said he deserved it and that I should call help. But I didn't. I was a scared coward who ran from the scene of the crime. But in that moment of escape, one of the bystanders outside must've called it in because several minutes later the sirens were ringing. I could hear them a couple blocks down as I rushed down the street and to the nearest bridge I could find. I stood there catching my breath, peering into oily-blue waters. I wanted to justify what had happened in 1971, but I couldn't. I would be exactly like him, a monster. And then when I told myself I would let go of the sharpened brush, it was already too late. I had become a monster like him. And now as I waited for the law to catch up, knowing that I couldn't hide, I wished for another way out. I couldn't jump; that was even worse than running away. There was only one way I could get out. One way that wouldn't make the guilt and shame worse, even though I would have to live with it for the rest of my life. I had to be better than Truci. Better than the darkness he had felt. I sat there, on the bridge, the madness already getting to my mind. I had caused the death of someone else."

"So you waited?" Andrea concluded.

"That's how I got here! I waited for the law to catch me and served what little time in prison I needed. I got what I deserved, Andrea. And then knowing I was never going to escape the madness, and guilt, I came here. It's only now after I'm released that I recall checking in to this hospital. The madness has ruined me, Andrea," fresh tears roll down my cheek.

She noticed and puts a hand on my arm. "You see, I think you persuaded the sun to come out," she said. And she's right; it's warmer than it was before. "Thank you for talking to me, Arthur! Do you ever plan on painting again?"

"I hate painting!" was all I could say.

"Oh I see! Bad memories have ruined it, haven't they?"

I didn't say anything as I looked up at the sun. "I tried to have a life, but I ruined it! And I think this is a lesson. Andrea, help others before they ruin theirs. Because I say it's not worth it. My mind falls to pieces whenever I try to be normal and not think about my past, but I'm having a hard time getting around that."

Andrea put the cap back on the thermos as I stand up to let her pack the table.

Before she can do anything about the chairs, I beat her to it before giving them to her.

"I know you'll get around, Arthur. I know you will. The cube might not leave you, and you can never leave the cube, but make the best of it!" she smiled innocently. And right there, right then, everything changed again. How did she know about the cube? I'd never told her.

"Who are you?"

The nurse looked back before departing from the roof, "I'm Andrea."

That left me stunned as she opened the fire door and went back to work. Now, and like many times in my life, I wanted to believe in prayer. I wanted to be able to communicate with a powerhouse of answers. To get questions answered that I'd always wanted answered. Questions like "What had she just admitted?" "Does God exist, and is the cube just a nightmare?"

The silent truth she had left me with was momentarily pushed aside as my latter question triggered a sudden reaction. I feel myself being pulled away from what was rooting me to the roof. And there above me is a bright, white light. My mind is playing tricks on me. The child in my head is punching the walls of it confinement like a boxing bag. It's causing a sharp pain in my head as I'm being picked up. *Somebody, help me down, please!* No one heard my thoughts as I rise up into the air. I was still standing, but then falling off balance, I lay on my back. It was like those science-fiction magazines that depict the victim being abducted by a UFO. Except, this was reality even though I was not sure if it's that at all. A reality where I'm a monster. The child in my mind, in the cube, has always called me that. But when I told Andrea about my past, it dawned on me. I can choose to be a monster if I want to, and I don't. The same goes for my sanity. I'm not insane; I'm not. But something, someone, is making it out to be. I was internally fighting the insanity someone else was bringing upon me. That conversation… it helped me discern if I was recovered or not. It also helped me realize I've always been recovered. The sky above, that wasn't a bright light, was drenched in that same dark, oily curtain like the waters under the bridge. The bright light in the dark sky shifted to a new scene as the carrying beam stopped and the sky swallowed me whole. I'm once again in the cube, and it was apparent I never left. Everything is exactly how it was when I was last here. The walls with their shades and mother, speaking to me in the tone I had come to know very well. I was a child again in this awful place. But something had changed. The voice of my mother, the grey wall, had changed. It was now replicated to personify an important person in my life. Of course, mother had never been a character of my life, or had she? The more I thought about it the more the voice seemed familiar. And then it dawned. The grey wall had sounded like my actual mother. The only distinction between the two was that the grey wall was nothing like I remembered her. The cube had taken a totally dissimilar form and mashed it together with a more negative approach to my mother's voice. And now that the cube was back, and I am more than sure that this couldn't be a dream or nightmare, that there had to be something very wrong. And it was proven next by my father's voice. The wall behind finally had an identity besides the word 'death' and 'Bright.' It was Grim. Grim, the cold-sounding father figure of my nightmare. He had been there for most of my life and now as I look back at the memories in my fractured mind, he made me who I am. Rather, he was one of them; Truci was also to be blamed.

"Hello, Arthur!"

Unlike the other times I was in the cube, I can fully move as I want. And so I turn to face Grim. I'm tired of not knowing what's real or fake. And I'm no longer afraid of these lies that are being fed into my consciousness. "Enjoy the insanity? Of course you don't!" he answered his own question as I stare at the wall that had taught me to fear. With a brief glance at the floor, I took note that it was once again a floor and not a gaping hole to be freed by. "You're resisting, Arthur! This is your reality, and you must live it!"

I rebelliously yell back, "No! This isn't real; it can't be!"

"Why can't it be? It looks real to me," he coaxed.

"The cube can't come back. This isn't reality. I know this ain't real because every time I know something's real, it isn't. You're playing a game that I've beaten you to. This ends now!"

"Fine, you got me!" the wall gave in as it turned into a white door. "Open the door; I know you want to! Open it to be freed!"

I don't answer as I hesitate to do as he says. I know it was most probably going to be another trick. Another dead end to getting out of wherever I was. But I have to try to find a loophole. And this is the only lead I have. Turning the glass doorknob, I entered the open door.

"At least, I don't have to listen to those annoying walls speak," I thought out loud.

This new world I stepped foot on was of sand. For as far as I could see, there was nothing but the dry powder that made up the ground. The door behind faded like ash from a flame. This was a never-ending prison. And there was no way out. Stretching out my arms, I talk to the sand, "Tell me, Grim, is this freedom? 'Cause I think you lied to me. This is a desert. And the only freedom I'm getting here is the freedom to dehydrate, and starve."

"What do you think? Is this freedom?" Grim chortled. "Is this all a lie? The answer, 'cause you'll never make it out, is yes? And the best thing is… this isn't even your life; it's mine. You must have my insanity. Become, become me!" The madman ranted away as I search for an invisible knob on the door that wasn't there.

I didn't know what to say, except, "You are exactly what you didn't want to be, Grim, a monster! You're planting your problems on someone else."

"No I'm not! I'm not a monster. Hear me? I'm not a monster!" Grim said becoming enraged while the sand rumbled under my feet.

"Only a monster would create the cube and it's walls!" I try as it might but the bitterness bled through.

"I didn't create the cube, Arthur! It's always been there. I've only shaped it to my design. And by the way, good luck with the sandstorm!"

"What sandstorm?" I regretted asking as the air became foul and the ground swirled up to clog my eyes and mouth.

"Oh and look, there's a door!" he informed me as I struggled for it at the other end of the desert. I run and then slow down, and then run again. And I finally get to the door, but not before it moves. It was now on the opposite end as the wind picked up pace. "Ah, it's gone, to the other side. You'll never make it, Arthur. Never! Remember the walls. All they said about you was right; you're useless," Grim chortled.

And then I change the direction I'm going in. But before I try to lessen the miles between the door and me, I get an idea. I continued the way I had been going.

"What a fool? You think…" The disembodied voice tries to discourage me as I feel myself returning to the hospital roof with a whooshing wind. The UFO is gone. Everything is how it was before Andrea brought me a conversation, and hot chocolate. The orphanage caretaker is gone. But it leaves me with a thought. What if I could rebel using Grim's matrix? Go where I want to, do what I want to do without constraints. I could choose my own fate instead of being the puppet under Grim's thumb. The real world doesn't work like this at all. Our fates and destinies are pre-chosen. Therefore, I run away because I can. Because I'm desperate for a loophole. I swing the fire door open and rush down the stairwell to the bottom floor. I pass the room where I had been kept to keep the story of the painter gone crazy, alive. I'm on the first floor, and whilst I weave through the busy corridors, I beg the cube to cloak eyes from seeing the ex-patient leaving. In turn, no one notices. But I am seconds away from being noticed as I enter the foyer and get to the front door. Theoretically, if Grim's puppets can't see me, neither can he. But theory in this case has nil effect when cheating is a part of the game. I attempt to open the front door, but I have no luck. Next to the door is a fire extinguisher strapped to the wall. With an unnatural strength brought on by the cube, I rip it from the brackets that kept it restrained. With it in both hands, I reel it back, and then hurl it at the glass that makes up the upper-half of the double door. I'm close to Freedom; I have to be. The fire extinguisher bounces off with not a scratch to the glass. There must be another way. Something that's out of the box. Something, like… I knew how to escape!

"I've figured it out! I know how to escape!" I automatically realize that my outburst was heard as the personnel of the hospital turn glaringly to me. Bolting into action, I run back through the main hallway and up to the second floor. The personnel already start to move toward me with crazed faces. However, halfway through the second floor's foyer, the cube's protective force broke.

The living mass of people around me chaotically screamed and then chased me through the rest of the last floor. I reached the stairway to the roof, but this time somebody was blocking the path. The path. She had died on the path. It was all my fault; I was the monster. I was the monster. Wait, no, I'm innocent.

"I'm innocent; let me go!" I ordered the darkened figure blocking my way up. It's evident now that I was doing the right thing, Grim was trying to stop me from enacting my final attempt at an escape. Wait, that can't be right, it's me. I'm blocking myself. The only way to stop him is to imagine he's not there. I'm ascending the steps now without any dithering and I feel him brush my shoulder. I'm no longer at the bottom of the stairwell and instead I'm the one blocking my exit. I see it now; he's putting doubt in my mind. That's why I can't be free. That's why the cube isn't mine. It's his. But I thought....

"You thought wrong, Arthur. You thought wrong," he looks up at me and says it with a voice not his own. But being the persistent person I am, I ignored him. I was so close to the roof. "Don't go that way, Arthur. You can't stop me; you can't escape. And you know you can't fight this; you won't fight this."

I ball up my fist like the day with Truci, but I resist giving in to the anger.

"I'm not a monster! I'm gonna fight this! I'm gonna escape! And I'm gonna stop you from whatever plan you have."

"You don't know the half of it!"

His message followed as I broke the hold and burst through the door. I collapsed on the rooftop from the hands that pulled me down. Like the horror it is, I'm being dragged into the stairwell by the cold hands of the puppets. I blindly kick and hear a cry as one leg is let go and then I pull myself back to the rooftop. I shake the last hands off and then shut the door. Then, I rush to the edge of the roof as it bursts open with the horde of zombie puppets. I'm so close now, I can feel it.

"You think this is going to change anything? You think you can escape the cube, 'cause you'll always be the child of the cube; you know that! Always, and there's nothing you can do," Grim taunts me from the nurse directly behind.

I turn and I know that the time for answers is now. It's Andrea. She was the first from all the other personnel to get to arm's length from my back.

"If I'm supposed to stay here in the cube, please tell me, did Andrea ever die?"

Silence, and then, "She did, but not in the forest. She got brain damage from the hit to the head, and passed slowly away. There was nothing I could do!"

Having nothing else to say, I tried to share his grief, "I'm sorry, Grim, for your loss."

"No, you're not, because no one cares. I was the only person at the funeral. This is the only way to make people care. That's right; you're not the only one."

"This isn't right, Grim. You can find other ways to get people to care," I tried to find good in the madman.

"No, I can't, Arthur! Puppets, attack him, now!" The puppet personnel grew closer with empty looks.

"You'll be stopped! 'Cause now I know what you're doing. And I'm leaving for the real world."

"We'll see about that, Arthur!" Grim's menacing, cold voice sent a shiver down my spine.

"Oh, I will escape! I'll escape wherever I am and I'll make sure you can't do any more harm to anybody!" I said as my arms were being grabbed and I'm being pelted with punches and kicks.

"Oh stop! You don't know anything! Remember the orphanage when I took you? You're still there! And that's not all that's there. He's there, too."

I'm getting flashbacks as I picture my family. Thereupon the truth breaks through Grim's world of madness. My brother Artimus and I were kidnapped from my parents. And now I' gonna return to them. I must.

"Oh, I know! I remember the real world now. You've been holding me in an abandoned orphanage since I was ten. I still am. That's what it means, child of the cube. It's what you do to all the children you kidnap. You imprison them in their minds by strapping them to this machine."

The horror was re-lived when a vision of my unconscious body being strapped to a movable chair and a cap being placed on my haired head, flashed before my eyes.

"You have done this to countless while their parents grieve. And you know why you did this? It's because you were orphaned young; someone killed your fiancé, and you found out you were working for him several years later as an apprentice. What do you have to say to that?" I asked as I grinned inside. I had finally found the bully's weakness, the truth. The world was covered in a veil of serenity and the zombie-like personnel behind me stopped. Blinking, I saw myself through a sheet of glass, but only as long as I didn't blink.

Grim had never recovered; he had run off from the hospital. I ran back to the fire door, and the madman must have thought I was changing my mind because the puppets were backing off. I wasn't. Instead, I was pulling back before releasing my plan. Andrea panicked. The puppeteer had finally figured out why I had loudly announced, "I figured it out!" downstairs.

"Don't! Please, don't! I promise I'll free you! I promise. But please don't tell me that. It's not my fault. It's all Truci, all Truci."

He had broken now as he spoke with the 'all-over-the-place' voice of a confused man.

"It can't be; Truci doesn't exist. My mother once taught me a tiny bit of Latin, and the word 'grim' was one of the words. Truci, means, you! You messed up the painter's identity to hide who it really was."

"Wow! You're a smart kid," Andrea menacingly smiled as I held my ready-to-run stance. "But you're right! I can't, after all, spill everything."

"Oh, and before I jump off the edge into reality, yes, this is entirely your fault. It's your fault for thinking you could outsmart a child," I was more than proud of myself as his final words blew away in the wind.

"No, you're a liar. I'm not the monster. It's not my fault! He did it; he did it! You are the monster, Arthur! You are!"

I ran off the edge of the rooftop as a cracking hole opened up in the sky and as Grim's minions turned to nothingness. If this was reality, I wouldn't have done it. Life is too precious to throw away. But it wasn't reality. I knew this because I was waking up from my bad dream to even more bad dreams. It was very true that I was the child of the cube. But you know what? The ones trapped in the orphanage, they're all children of the cube. We're all the children of the cube and today the madness would end. Today, it was going to be a happy ending for all of us. No more mind games and nightmares of the things that had happened. The time had come for Grim and his world of madness to end. It was time for the children to be free.

YELLOW

In the world of Block, there was more than the purple silhouette and the annoying parasite he called The Intruder. They had been battling out control over the planet, on a mountain overlooking a wide expansion of forestry, ocean, and smaller patches of desert. Yet there was even more to be seen apart from this and the only city on a dirt flatland, rimmed by lively, green trees. Not to mention, there was a little hut that smoked away at the foot of the mountain. No, there was even more life on the planet than the Intruder's poor imitations of the native species. And at the exact moment when the installed personalities were uploaded to Block, another human found out what Dr. Wigget had. She had been robbed of her old self. And unlike the Purple Dot, she was another colour, and a totally inhuman shape. Arik Summers would have a new name any moment now. A name very similar to that of her colleague's. Instead of purple, she would be yellow, and not a dot. She was at first nothing. Nothing, as in the air you breathed, and the gases that are subjected to that air. Now the introduction of a certain detective by the Intruder's power had simultaneously split itself into three villains. Three separate from the one above and now one of them had taken refuge at the very bottom of an outcropping of mountains. An outcrop that was to the north and a ways off from the virus and the dot. This ensured the virus' continuation and made it much harder to eradicate it. If only the natives of Block had known what they were really up against. If only they knew beforehand that the destruction of the three spawns would leave the main entity weakened. But no worries, Arik Summers, Yellow, would find the first spawn. She would find it with the help of what defense Block had for her. And since the spawn couldn't be an enemy without a name, and a matching appearance, it chose one. He had taken on the form of a full tea cup. By tea cup, I mean that he looks like your typical white china cup with the embellished designs a grandmother would favor. The cup's name, fitting the description, was Tea. Mr. Tea had hatched his own devious plan to take over the world if the Intruder's plan wasn't enough. A plan that his superior found childish and stupid. But it wasn't a stupid plan in his tea cup eyes. It detailed the act of taking all the air in the barren world and replacing it with tea. This would be a step for domination, a back-up to ensure the virus would succeed. The back-up would take the gift of breathing away from the original inhabitants. It would also be adapted to make them more like what the virus wanted and less than what they used to be. The new humans would no longer be human, and therefore this would foil Dr. Wigget's vision of Block. Besides, oxygen was useless to Tea. He didn't need to breathe at all. He was technically not even alive compared to the others living on the planet. And to top that off, he couldn't freely move around. His view didn't include how the world really looked like outside. He only had the scenery that he saw from his room's window. Yes, seeing beauty was constricted to only the tower that was positioned inside a circlet of mountains not too far away from the smoking house. The reason for the lack of movement was of course the obvious. He had no legs. The story behind why he had nothing to hold him up fit between his beginning and now. Not long ago when The Intruder created the three spawn, Tea had found where he wanted to set-up home. The cup had designed it to be a small castle crammed into a tall column. Time went differently below the mountain, opposed to on the mountain; it didn't take long for Block's security to catch wind of the nesting pest. It had fantasized a match for the cup. A match or a blood-thirsty hippo. The cup had lost badly when it's legs were no more, bitten off by the pink hippo. Then with a final swig, the heavy, four-legged creature swallowed the pair whole. To this day it had been given a name by the victim, the Legeater. The rest of that dreadful story ended with a miserable Mr. Tea in a tower he couldn't explore. He dragged himself up the stone stairwell and to the highest point, and has stayed there ever since. It was on a dull, cloudy day that he speculated on what his life could possibly be missing. He had everything he wanted, except… maybe he needed a chance to be superior. To be able to feel the responsibility of leading. That was it; he needed minions. And so sitting there by the window, he wished for this, when an accident occurred. He had no idea of the power he had, until now. With a flick of his handle, he accidentally spilled a bit of ordinary, sugared tea. That puddle, to his surprise, became two things of interest. Things old earth called spoons. Blank-faced, crooked-nosed, and grinning with purpose. They were also spotted with puny, black eyes that didn't help with their appearance. Mr.Tea immediately saw this as a wish come true from his father. They were his minions. He also believed that this was a warning that meant his life would become threatened at any moment. The spoons were to be his bodyguards. They awaited his command until he spoke of what he wished them to do. He knew how he was going to replace the air with tea. Now having an inkling of his power, he poured some of his tea into several procured vials. Next, he vaporized the liquid inside with pure willpower, before giving the vials to the spoons. They exited the room and went down the flight of the stairs to the rocks below. Mr. Tea was once again alone, and the back-up plan had been set into action.

As soon as the spoons touched the ground with their foot, or their stump of a leg, they got to work. They opened their vials simultaneously to let out a small portion of the tea before closing it and disappearing into nothingness. The sky became a light haze of chamomile-yellow and in a minute or so, or several seconds later, the sun was no more. This was happening all over the lower parts of Block as the two minions were carrying out their terrible task. That disappearance before had merely been teleportation replacing the humans' long-destroyed polluting machines. Long-destroyed along with a dead planet. This was transportation at its finest. [6]And this meant no climate change. But with the yellowy haze burning in the air, the polar bears and ice would surely die sooner than before. But

---

6 I am currently at a no man's land position when it comes to climate change. I am unsure whether to agree or disagree. The wanting to agree thanks to pictures and videos is great, but the wanting to disagree still plagues my indecisive mind. The same goes with my caring about the situation. I care about the world and so if this is actually happening then I think we should do something about it. But if it's all a conspiracy, a lie, then please leave me alone. And here's an idea for you. What if the end of the world, the apocalypse, is our fault? In this case, climate change may very well be the end. It may be our end and the question is what can two disagreeing sides do? I don't really know. Only time will tell. On the other side, this concept of two disagreeing sides is very familiar to the second story in this book.

then again, what were Block's polar bears like? And ice, did Block have ice?

They finished polluting, but there was still one thing standing in their way. The living planet they were trying to manipulate. A planet with an AI, a consciousness. And like any living thing, it's bound to fight back when it feels endangered. So in order to get rid of Tea and his bizarre plot, the planet generated its own bodyguard. It chose a program from Block's control center underneath the surface, and using a cloud from the polluting sky, gave it a body. Arik Summers was given a new form. From out of all the consciousness' she was picked because before earth died out, she was a trusted friend of Dr.Wigget. Dr.Wigget had been the first consciousness to be activated to stop the virus, The Intruder, from taking over the planet and mutating it to its own will. The light-yellow beverage crossed with the lines that figured together to form a yellow cloud. And as she became the cloud, she was instantly informed by Block of the situation at hand, and The Intruder. She knew she had been sent to stop Tea and his minions but she didn't have a clue how. The chamomile gas overrode the oxygen around Yellow while she investigated her surroundings. Hovering over a narrow stream of water that snaked through the base of the mountain, she looked down. There it was, the coordinates, a guiding light to where she had to go. It was an arrow that pointed at the mountain wall. But, there was nothing there. *Unless*, she thought about the possibility of a secret passage. "Nah," she doubted and perceived it as impossible. Because she didn't want to believe there was something hidden behind the wall, she went her own way. Searching the farscape of the forest from the top of the tallest tree, she spotted them. The spoons were down at a western beach where the forest ended, only to swoop around this small part of the encompassing ocean that dominated Block. The swooping trees and ground ended enough for a wide opening of water to spill through into the bigger body. Yellow hovered there above the trees while the spoons released more of their gas. When they had finished, she followed slowly, making sure she stayed out of their sight. Following was almost made impossible when the intended target could teleport, but she made do as best as she could, still failing multiple times. They would disappear; she would lose them, and then she would search, and find them again, and it went like that several times. But it all added up to the three making it back to the tower. And this time, Block's message finally made sense to Yellow. She had been wrong to disobey a simple prod in the right direction. An arrow that pointed to the mountain wall, which hid what she had first thought was a secret passage, had been ignored. She had gone her own way like the Israelites from long ago.

"We would rather go back to being slaves than being chased down by the Egyptians!"

"Yeah! I would rather be a slave than walk in the middle of nowhere in the hot and snake-infested desert."

"Are you sure you heard a fiery bush talk? That isn't even a thing. How can you believe he exists and still loves us after abandoning us to the natives of Egypt?"

"He said we were supposed to be a blessing to them. But how can you be a blessing to those who treat you like yesterday's trash?" They all took turns questioning and complaining. Moses would just shake his head in annoyance at them and their whining. He tried to tell them and to get them to trust him, but it was useless. And then when the Egyptians had drowned in the Red Sea, they were happy again. The complaints had gone.

"Bubble, bubble, there goes our slavers. Goodbye, sweet dreams!" One of the Israelites leaned over the sea with a grin and wave. But that wasn't the end of their complaints. No, that was just the beginning. Not just for complaints, but bad luck. Yes, the Israelites were going to have some very bad luck. And like Moses being annoyed at them, Yellow knew that even though Block didn't say a thing, it was just a little bit disappointed in her. Yellow followed the minions as they came closer to the wall with the stream. The mountain-side shook and it parted to reveal a pathway. The stream moved to the side of the path that in turn pooled up by the tower. Open at the top like the hidden valley it was, you could see Block's only sun and the unaffected sky. The spoons wound down the way to the tower. Once the spoons had disappeared through the tower's only door, Yellow, still at a swift pace, floated briskly upward to avoid detection. Upward to Tea's window where she hovered, picking up the conversation and what she could see. She hadn't even heard the first fleck of talk when Arik came across a thought. *This vapor is made of chamomile. Which means, it can put its breathers to sleep*, she thought. *I mean, I wouldn't know because I don't need to breathe.* Then she asked the planet, and he confirmed her theory. But so far, no one had been put to sleep, or had suffocated from the lack of oxygen. Through the window, Yellow saw Tea as he admired his work of art. Tea's speckled-gray eyes came across an emptying thought as they drooped down. By the way he held himself, Arik could tell he was self-absorbent. And knowing that he was the first spawn, it made total sense. To him, something was still missing. So he added a glorious ocean of waves that made the tear even more beautiful to look at.

"Tear, what a wonderful word!" he said to himself, not knowing that someone was listening. "Air plus tea shall surely need a new name. For it is not neither, but both." Then he fell over a change, a new combination. "Ah hah! Tea and then air minus the AI. Soon, you won't be the same, Block; you'll be ours, all ours. And my creation, Tea, will be the new oxygen. The separate tears my minions have released will put Dr.Wigget's people to sleep and rewrite their breathing biology." The white China cup grew silent. Then for the rest of the day he went on gazing at the work of art he had created, until a knock came at his door. Turning sharply around, he was distracted from his Van Gogh. The outside had the same bleeding effect in which everything looked to be slightly smudged. Not just that, but with the outside like waves, it looked like swirls as the colours through it were brightened. The beauty outside had been made with invisible brush strokes. "Come in!" he said gruffly. The door opened with a loud swish and he was greeted by two frightened spoons. "What is it? What's the matter?" a caring but urgent question availed.

"I think we're being followed, sir!" the tallest spoon answered.

"By whom or what?"

"By a yellow cloud, sir! It's been following us since we got back from the western bay," the other one spoke with a deeper voice.

"And what exactly do you think it wants?" Mr. Tea was now privately considering that he might have to vanquish his minions. This stalker of theirs had to be a work of fiction. It had to be. Unless Legeater was back. Now he worried and Yellow smiled at this. She knew about the hippo. The only way she knew about it was because Block had told her.

The tallest of the two minions and the first to speak came back to the conversation.

“I think it was trying to eat us, sir,” it said. “What shall we do?” they asked in unison.

“Nothing! We shall do nothing! ’Cause it’s a lie and you’re both fools!” the cup ignorantly laughed off what they had to say. But underneath it all was a quickening worry. It was back; it had to be. A scowl added to his ignorance, which led to the spoons leaving his company. They would go attend to things in another part of the tower. It was that simple; they were there and then not. Their use was starting to expire now that the gas was doing its work. But the story of the cloud nagged the cup. That silly story he had heard wasn’t true; it couldn’t be. Tea sighed and went back to admiring the Van Gogh. Yellow, still listening and watching, moved further up. This was her chance to confront the spawn. It was her turn to prove the cup wrong. It doesn’t just give normal, white clouds. It gives yellow clouds too. The cloud floated down and into the chamber as Tea backed away. “You’re real! I can’t believe it! You’re actually standing right in front of me. Or should I say, floating right in front of me.” He had been caught off guard. Arik knew he had.

The cloud gave him a stone-serious look that asked the real question. Her bead-like eyes aided the way she intimidatingly asked him the question. The question that had been burning inside her since her rebirth.

“Why have you destroyed the atmosphere? The very oxygen the people breathe is now murky and polluted. Their existence is threatened!”

“Hmm, so be it! After I take over every inch of air, they won’t be the same, and I promise you that.” The cup and the cloud met in the center.

"You can try to stop me as much as you want, but you'll fail. Fail, fail, fail! And we'll win, win, win! Spoo...," but his call was interrupted.

"Without a question, you're full of yourself, Tea! I know Dr.Wigget gave The Intruder a chance. And I'll give you another one before Block stops you from taking our air. Change it now, before I do what the Purple Dot couldn't!"

"No! I will not," Mr.Tea was just as resilient as his superior. "You know what to do, Yellow! The only way you're going to change what's happening is by swallowing my life whole. You're a cloud! You can absorb me and all the chamomile gas on the planet goes. You can save everyone." The cup had changed in an instant. He was now supporting his own demise and Yellow could see that the only way to stop the cup was what he said. So Yellow played along with what she feared was a trick.

"The downside to that would be that your Van Gogh would be ruined forever. Are you sure you want me to take beauty away from you?"

The cup gulped, spilling a droplet of tea, "Yes, I suppose; that's a good question. Because all true artists know that their own personal Van Goghs, are in their...," the cup pointed to the brain he didn't have. "Which sadly, I don't have. So I guess I don't want it to go after all. But it must, it must be destroyed. I cannot live; Mr.Tea cannot be alive," he grew still.

Arik Summers grinned and did something her human self would never do.

"That's what I thought," she finalized the non-existent deal. Her thin line of a mouth widened till it could fit a round-ish item within its realm. Then she finished what Legeater should have done long ago. Make Mr. Tea disappear. The Yellow cloud swallowed the cup before he could say another thing. The Van Gogh outside, however, didn't go away. She took a long breath that she didn't need, but it still stayed. It had been a trick and she said to herself she wouldn't take the bait. You never say never 'cause it always goes the other way. Or at least, a lot of the time. "That's what I thought! A piece of the virus is attacking this planet for the humanity it has. I mean that; it wants to be human. It wants to be the only human in existence."

"It's true. I'm embarrassed now. You found out something about me."

Yellow looked at her stomach, "What do you want with me?"

"Don't panic, Yellow! I'm going to become you. It was the only way to get rid of you. And now, that immunity the planet gave you, against me, has been corrupted. Hear that, Block; it ends with the fighting back. First with Legeater, now her. You, Yellow, are going to become brush strokes on my world. You will be tea, like me!" he rhymed as he became himself again in form.

"No, I will not!"

"Don't make the mistake Purple Dot did! Oh, and by the way, it'll soon be too late! The tea will take you over!"

"Why, you!" she came closer.

"Spoons!" his yell bounced around in the tower and it wasn't long before they came. Yellow hid herself from view of the open door. And before Mr.Tea could warn the spoons, she took the only chance she would ever get. Dark-yellow tendrils popped out of the cloud and grabbed the shortest spoon by its stumped leg. Then, like she was playing a game of baseball, she batted the only ball she could see. The cup smashed to a thousand shards, which fell everywhere but close to Yellow. Then as that happened, the tea contained inside went everywhere. Like a flood, it washed the cloud back through the window and flat on the stone rocks below. All she saw as she spun around was the aiding spoons as they came to their master's side, but all that fizzled to nothingness as the entire tower melted away. Everything that The Intruder's spawn had done failed to exist. Arik took in everything for a moment. Then something in the distance caught her eye. Something was falling out of the sky, and she had a feeling she knew what it was. Too caught up in the rescue she was gonna attempt, the cloud never took a long look at herself. She was no longer yellow, but white. As white as a cloud should be. Racing out of the valley of mountains, she skimmed back over the trees of Block, and caught the falling dot. Dropping him gently to the ground with her long tendrils, she hovered there as he picked himself up. He acknowledged where he had fallen and looked back at the mountain, following its ascent with his eyes.

"I suppose you're probably one of The Intruder's creations," the Purple Dot had the face of someone who was weighed down by responsibility.

"Intruder, what intruder?" Yellow tried to be humorous by pretending The Intruder didn't exist, but the fallen dot just glared at her. "Do you mean?" she went on, still attempting humor, and pointed in the direction of where the tower used to be. "No; I'm sorry, he went that way."

"You don't think I'm fooled by that, do you? You know who I'm talking about because you're here to make sure I'll never be able to get Block back." His head drooped with eyes at his feet. He sounded more than hopeless.

"Would one of The Intruder's minions save you, Henry?"

His head shot up at this and a smile of recognition was plastered on his purple face. "Arik! You were always terrible with humor. But I just can't believe you're truly here. The planet must have chosen you to help me, but why?"

"Yeah it's me, Henry! And yes, the planet did choose me to help you. But not how you think. The Intruder divided himself into three extra spawns to root himself in place. We have to foil all three in order to defeat it."

"Where are we gonna find these spawns?"

"I've already taken care of one, a tea cup by the name of Mr.Tea. He had these spoons for bodyguards and he wanted to take all of the air away and replace it with a gas he created from himself. He called it the chamomile gas. Can you believe all that, Henry?"

"It is hard to, yeah, but I get it. That's what we have to do, and our best shot at finding the second spawn is up there," he motioned to the mountain. "I'm presuming Block told you everything?"

She nodded. "He never showed me what the virus looks like."

Wigget tried to keep the giggling back, but it was too much. "He copied me. Then he turned into *the* detective."

"No," she burst into her own fit of giggles and laughs.

"I couldn't take him serious at all."

"I believe it," Yellow said as they calmed down and went back to what they were going to do. "And our only chance, Henry Wigget, is to get up the mountain; you're right."

"Then you know we better get moving," Dr. Wigget suggested.

"Though you know, Henry, I'm not a mountain climber. I never was. I mean 2005, yes. But I was going through a phase. Anyway, I better stay behind."

Henry glanced back at her in a jest smile, "Arik, you're a flipping cloud. You could float up there in no time. Hah, there's an idea!"

"What?"

"I'm only 170 pounds and you're a cloud," Henry Wigget hinted to an already forming idea.

"You want me to lift you up?" disbelief crossed Arik's voice.

"Yeah, why not? I mean, my arms are going to get tired eventually but we can always take a break."

"I can't say no, can I?" Arik asked, not really wanting to say no.

"Not really, no. I need your help, Arik. I can't stop the virus without you."

"Okay then, let's go. It's starting to get dark anyway, and we should've already started headin' up."

Doctor Henry Wigget jumped onto the cloud's back as he held on for dear life. What a sight it was as the two figures floated their way up the mountain while the sun was drooping down into the new earth. "So what do you call yourself now, the Purple Dot? Because that would be something," she teased. But Dr. Wigget didn't answer back.

Then as they ascended, he sang a song. "I'm a little tea cup, short and stout…."

0I000002IIIIIII000002IIII000002IIII200000000IIII000002IIIIII000002IIIIIIII,:

THE CATHOLIC HITMAN

Paloma Park, the only place where a thousand year-old fountain resided. Or that's what everyone said, though the man doubted it. He knew one thing in this world, one thing he didn't doubt. That one thing was that everything ends, and today he had a choice. His feet made footprints in the snow as he entered the archway to the church wall. And then taking off where it left, stone steps arose, leading into a whole new layer of relic stonework. He made his way up the steps with the large, black case. Movement was evident in his dark-brown hair as it thrashed around on his head, his eyes the colour of jade and his waxy features unaffected by the motion he was enduring. Today was like any other day, except his mind was tossing and turning with something he had left with his past. At the end of the steps, he turned onto another set of stairs and embarked until he was eventually at the highest level of the stone building.

Now, what was the perfect place for an end to be committed? "That's simple," he thought to himself, silence still sitting on his lips. "That narrow slit in the wall that overlooks the park of naked trees and snow. Not just that, but humans walking in their own lives."

[7]This was a day in the life. And it being a special time of the year, the park was dressed in colourful lights, and carolers sang their favorite songs. The park, it could be said, was merry as everyone enjoyed themselves with the festivities. Festivities of warm drinks, baked goods, singing, and opening presents under a decorated tree. The man settled by the wall, making sure to stay out of prying and wandering eyes. Then he began to unpack the gift. The long, narrow box was surely to be a good gift. The thing was he hated it. It wasn't life; it was surely death. The thing he had left behind in his past was coming back. As a child, he had grown up in a home where faith was important. But what stopped it was that his father had no heart for it. He didn't believe in hope or anything related to religion. The man's father was in no better words, a cold man.

He was heartless and didn't care. He was the weed that had started the man's profession. The man and his mother despised their father and husband even though they loved him. And so, it was sad when he died of overdosing on whatever the doctors believed it was. To say it straight, drugs killed him. It didn't matter how the man thought of it; it had torn the family in two. Not to mention, he had lost a brother to brain cancer shortly after. Thereafter, it wasn't easy, but he had survived a short time before finding an occupation that killed him as well. Life wasn't important to him and death was the only result. He believed the purpose of living was to die. And so he ended the lives of bad people. Humans that did worse things that he

---

7 Song suggestion: A day in the life by The Beatles

himself had done. He was a hitman. It wasn't something to be proud of; it wasn't a video game. This was all real. So what did this mean? Was the hunt on? This whole time he had been piecing together the weapon, and now it had been finished. He had finalized it by attaching the hulky capsule, but something kept him from setting it on the base of the arching space in the wall. It also happened that the religion his mother, brother, and himself had stuck to before he became what he was now, was emerging once again to question what he was doing. This man used to be a Catholic. And at some point of his life, he had come to the conclusion that he could cover up the pact he had made. He was starting to finally realize that once a Catholic, always a Catholic. But the thing that really bugged him was his position to determine justice for whoever needed justifying. The thought he had stuck to for so long was that he was doing this for the greater good. It wasn't the money he achieved by ridding others' targets; it was the act of cleansing the world of sin. But surely it was a sin to kill, to take another human's life. So to him, this profession was a sin. It was a sin to eradicate sin because he didn't have the right. The only one who could judge was God. Why then, was a mortal acting as judge and executioner? In his mind, he was a good guy helping his father, but in reality, he was a villain and a nuisance. At the end of the day, he would have made the decision of either being good or bad, or hero or villain. In the present moment, something or someone was to die. And it was between his corrupted path, and the continuation of that path. The weapon was slowly set on the stone where empty space took refuge. Then, he put his eye to the scope and a dominant finger ready at the trigger. The man he was hunting had recently been freed from prison on a charge of multiple homicides. He was, in fact, a retired general that had ruined his life by purging it of everyone that had done him wrong. When he was serving in the Vietnam War, he had taken the lives of several fellow soldiers due to his hatred toward them. Out of all these reasons the hitman had to make the criminal go away, the greatest was that he looked like his father. His crimes were much different from the Catholic's father, but the resemblance was uncanny. It was almost unreal and most certainly a nightmare. And in a hitman's vision, nightmares have no place in the world, besides themselves, of course. The scope focused on a figure that was making its way through the park at a leisurely pace. It grew in shape to reveal a bald-headed man that was dressed rather fashionably in a gray, tweed jacket. Or at least it used to be fashionable. Now it was instead a tattered segment of his reflection and the rest of his garments helped to prove that the general wasn't doing as well as he could have. Footwear was evidently coming to an end as his shoes showed age and his trousers drew eyes with their ripped up material. This man wouldn't be missed if a mortal playing God would end his miserable life. It would benefit him. But the hitman's mother would have doubted that very much. And nonetheless what she doubted, the Catholic hitman deemed the man unworthy to live. Not just that, but he had been given a contract from someone in the government, someone who despised the general for his cowardice personality. The once-superior to the homicidal maniac. So in other words, the hitman had no real reason for wanting the man dead, the government did. Everything he knew about the general and the judgement he held had been all based on what the official had told him. The official being the deputy to the prime minister of the government. The hitman didn't even know the target and from what he had heard there was no doubt that the figure down below was indeed a bad man. But what about the Catholic? Wasn't he also a bad man? He himself had killed many people, so what gave him the right? This had all been a mistake to take part in, but what the official had said sounded like this was something that had to be done. He had said this was the right thing to do. It wasn't though, and the Catholic hitman knew it. But he had no choice. If he didn't do what the government wanted, they would have to throw him away with other criminals. And if he did what they said, they would either forget about him even being there, or again, imprison him with the guilty. So really there was no contract, no money, only a hollow choice. But wait, it wasn't totally about the future. Instead, it had to do with faith and his religion. He was what he was and he had to take that into account. Would he go to prison with another life lost by his hands no matter how evil this life was or is? Or, would he go to prison knowing he let an evil man out into the world? The thought of prayer coursed through the processes of the hunter, but he acknowledged that time was of the essence and he believed the truth was nearby. He believed after some thought that he couldn't do God's work.

And like his mother had said some years before she too had passed, "The only judge is no one on this world." Truth was that he was at a loss at what to do. He was in a battle where three endings existed simultaneously. He could win, lose, or do neither. Win or lose. His finger inched closer to the trigger and his scope followed evil's travel. Time was running out! The hourglass of sand almost full. That face of his father, the one that had treated him like nothing, he wanted it to fall more than anything. The evil and the many terrible memories. The many nightmares and the scars that left the son to wander in the dark, still knowing he was being watched. This was a temptation for the quieting of a nightmare. Time ticked by, the struggling hunter checked his watch, almost three. Was it possible the government would try to silence the rebel? He rephrased that in his thoughts, was it possible they would try again? Hire another hitman or assassin that had no ties to religion? This way, his killing hands wouldn't be halted by the question of justice. And maybe, just maybe, instead of throwing the good sinner away, they would bury him in a coffin. His gravestone would have no title as in who died. They would shrug their shoulders when others asked, telling them he was a nobody. Guess what, everyone's a nobody until they evolve to somebody. And this man, wasn't a nobody. This man was a human, faults attached. Sinner or perfectionist, he was a somebody. A somebody that proved you could come back from losing your heart and soul. He was the good guy of his job, the only one. Better than he had made himself out to be. A wolf in sheep's clothing. Maybe this was right, maybe wrong. One thing's for sure; we're about to see what happens. Does it give a Catholic hitman? The switch happened from watch to an eye against the scope, with the hand back by the trigger. With one sign of compression, it would release a poison through the air. A poison of copper, carrying Cain's strand of sin. It had moved. The target was now sitting at a bench and in both hands he was holding a black object with his head down in concentration. This was it; the bad guy knew what had to be done. Faith or no faith, a job was a job. He pulled the trigger and that was the end of a living soul. The weapon was quickly folded back into the black box while the guilty man hid from sight. By now, the people in the park would have heard the sound and matched it to the dead body. They would automatically assume that the carcass had once been a nuisance to somebody. All he knew was that the government would be very reactant to this, and he was alright with that. They were, after all, merely mortals, not gods. Finishing his task at hand, he arose a little too quickly. The hitman looked to the park for finalization of theory before advancing to the steps. When he glanced at the circle of living forms crowding the deceased, he noticed that one figure wasn't with the others. It was the first mistake that had happened in his profession. The locking of eyes and an acknowledgement that the figure understood. Then like nothing happened, they both went back to what they had been doing. Steps ended and more travel occurred before the final set of steps announced themselves. His hand came up to raise the collar on his coat aside from the small change of a bowed head. Nobody noticed him as he made his way out of the park. His destination, a cozy apartment where a cup of hot cocoa warmed December away. It had been a cold day and he had learned something. Today was the last day. He didn't know the consequences, but whatever they were he would wait at his home. All he could do was hope they would understand and forgive. It was Christmas after all. A quick thought awakened action and he was at the side of the man he had seen before.

"The apartment I live in is just across from here. I would be tickled if you came over for supper," the hitman said and started to leave but then added another point to the invitation. "It's door number seven on the second floor," he nodded and the hitman took this as his time to leave.

"Anytime?" the invited man questioned with uncertainty.

"Yeah, anytime!" he answered. The Catholic, now no longer who he used to be, was changed. His part was done, so he headed home. To this day, no one besides them has the foggiest notion of what happened that evening. All went supposedly well and both men went their own ways once again. It was Christmas and one bad guy couldn't let the other have a day of loneliness. Everything had turned out better than the Catholic hitman had thought it would at the beginning of the day. There was still a crowd of people where an incident had formed. However, it was dissipating quickly. Nothing more could be done; nature had done its thing, and no ambulance would be called today. Things like this sorted themselves out until nothing was evident. The crowd was now gone except the man who had seen the one responsible. Seeing the one with the cap and coat up in the abandoned relic of a building told him that he should be very thankful. This day could have ended with a different type of dying. His life had been at stake and now he was questioning the result. The theory he held was that the man had spared his life due to the black book. He was holding his theory. That man had been a bad man, and so had he. But he knew this Christmas would be very different from the last. He knew this because he had met someone who was similar. He could just tell by the way the hitman had looked at him. They shared something that was stronger than both of them combined. Their religions and their ugly pasts. The sitting ended and he was now standing. Closing the book, he started walking in the same direction as the other had. Along the way, he passed the fallen victim. This was Paloma Park, so therefore, the stranger had still committed a wrong. The Catholic hitman had killed a pigeon. The general gently pushed the dead bird onto the grass, keeping it from being stepped on. Then he draped his bald head with a navy-blue toque, and was off. He had begun the day thinking that his life could be taken away at any moment due to his past. But the thing was it hadn't been taken, not yet anyway. His second chance was finally starting to be clear to him. He couldn't forget the things he had done, but he could change, he really could. That man had been after him, not the bird. But what changed this? The general glanced down at the Bible as he exited the Spanish park. We people can change; that's what one man discovered today.

000002III00000IIIII20000IIIII2000002I000002II:

TIME ARK

France was a dreary and wet time of ze year. It had so far been a miserable day. Hoping for excitement in ze silly humans of zis pompous and arrogant city, my body sat on its cold seat. I needed something that would better my miserable ailment. My seat though, overlooked ze perfect little street and a row of side-by-side houses. I had been sitting here for a while now, but nobody had walked by. Ze sky went dark until night was upon my red iris. Still no one came to heal ze symptoms of a bad day. Ze weather was terrible, my feathered friends were busy doing feathered things, and I had been unable to find any type of sustenance because some stupid feathered friends took it and swallowed it whole. Zose feathered friends, I tell you. I was about to leave the now-warming seat, when I saw ze perfect thing. Ze darkness of ze day, I knew, would be washed away from ze flood of zis man's life. Ze short, clean-shaven, and white-powder wigged man walked down ze street with a long face. He had also, I presumed by zis upside smile, been having a horrible, terrible, very stinky day. In his dirty hands was a large wad of paper that fell from his grasp and sprawled on the cobblestones below. He bent to pick them up one by one and zen once he had collected ze black-lined parchments, he cursed a certain establishment, and continued on ze hurried walk. "Zat blithering theater. Zey will feel what I have to say about rejecting my script. It would have been wonderful. So wonderful zat people would have come from overseas to see it and understand nil. Now I will make zem shudder at ze sound of my name, Joshua Vivuer!" ze small man vehemently promised.

"Ahh," I happily sighed. This was ze start to ze entertainment I needed to lighten my mood. Today was ze first of spring and my bad day would soon be cured. Vivuer and his papers of what I now knew was a script, kept walking further, and further along the cobblestone. Suddenly, however, he stopped mid step as ze cool air bit at me and I could see he was growing colder as he started to hug himself with his tweed coat. It was no longer raining and thank ze watcher of all animals for zat. Ze cold was enough as my bottom was warmed by ze seat till ze point where if I sat too long I would surely burn. Ze failing playwright stood in a confused terror that grew and grew in his eyes as he gripped the play tightly in his arms. First, he mumbled words I could barely make out. Zen he spoke louder till his words were too loud not to notice.

"Get out of my way!" he mumbled quietly, zen. "Wait, no! Demon, leave me alone! Zat colourful dress does not amuse me!" He pointed a finger at something I couldn't see. Joshua ended his shouting. Zen he spoke again, more calmer zis time, more reasonable. "Why should I believe you zat you come from another time, earlier than my own?" A break took place as he waited for an answer. "You say it doesn't matter if I believe you or not? Well, good to know; I do not. I believe zat I'm either out of my endearing mind or you are in fact from ze heavens above. Or ze hells below. If you are from ze heavens, please accept my apology for calling you a demon. I mean no disrespect," another break happened to what I assumed was in actuality ze figure answering what ze Frenchman had to say. "So zis time, Egypt. In what you call, 1526 B.C you're a baka. Ah, I see! A king's male heir. So you're a prince. And with a sparkly headdress like zat, I see you're no liar. My fear, I see now, was very illogical. You are not frightening, but rather I would say fascinating, Mr.Amenhotep." Ze conversation between the past figure and Vivuer was most illuminating. So much zat I was already feeling ze misery fade from my life. Ze invisible prince asked the want-to-be playwright his title. "I am," he took his time thinking of what to say to this foreigner. "I am Joshua Vivuer, ze greatest playwright zat has ever existed in France! And yes, if you have travelled across timelines for a very good script, I am, how zey say, ze right man for ze job. I just want to know… how can you speak French if you are from another place in ze world where zey don't speak French?" "So you say zat you have been captured by what zis machine calls itself a time ark? I suppose zen you say zat zis machine puts you in a time period and zerefore you are connected with zat era and zat place? You speak ze same language and dress similar. Zat makes a strange sense. You want me to free you? You do; zen how do I do so? How do I free you from zis time ark?"

Ze suspense was putting me on ze edge of my seat. How could Mr. Vivuer free ze prince from his prison? And was ze time ark on its own agenda or was it in ze hands of someone a little more human? Vivuer repeated his question, "How can I save you from whatever doom zis time ark has for you?" Ze prince was apparently disappearing from ze sight of ze Frenchman. "No, please! I want to help you. Just tell me how? How do I free you from ze ark?" I could tell it was too late. For zat desperate face he had had was replaced by ze frown of before. He started to walk again as ze street parted from ze row of houses and a Victorian bridge replaced it. To keep up with zis drama, I moved on to a different perch, still as warm for my buttocks as before. Mr. Vivuer looked over ze bridge into a moon-lit river. Mumbling once again to himself, he stared dreamily into ze waters. Ze center of my attention drowned out ze noises of carriages as zey travelled in ze dead of night. Zat was ze only sound except for insects zat harbored by ze waters of ze bridge. Zese sounds of insects were so loud zat my stomach was rumbling and I realized after so long zat I was hungry. Timing ze opening of my mouth, I caught a large fly zat went down rather nicely. Vivuer looked up at ze heavens with a mixture of a new horror. Something was happening. He was seeing one of the ark's apparitions again. "Is zis your doing, Amenhotep? Is zis flying carriage, with flames, is it yours? Is it part of ze time ark? And it hasn't a horse!" he shielded his eyes and zen looked over his shoulders.

The flying carriage had vanished as soon as it had appeared. "I suppose zat was ze future. Wasn't it?" A drunken civilian walked by, startled by ze conversant Vivuer.

"It was the future!" my ears heard a voice I couldn't ignore. It was coming from behind Joshua. He turned around to face it.

"Who are you?" he asked in his deepest French.

"I am Lincoln, Abe Lincoln." Ze voice disappeared and I could see ze figure now, accent-less, and wearing a black top hat. But zat, too, disappeared. "You asked how to free us. Lose the script!

That's how!" Ze voice was back, and zen in a flash I saw ze black-suited figure before it walked back ze way Vivuer had come from.

"What does it mean, Lincoln? What does it mean?"

Ze figure looked back to ze Frenchman. "Use the script! It's time-changing, quite literally. It's...," Abe Lincoln fizzled away before our eyes, leaving ze confused Frenchman to stand by ze edge of ze bridge. He stood there for a long time, and finally I decided I would shout at him. Shout with my language. Ze language my feathered friends shared. He glanced at me, and zen he understood. He understood what I said. Mr.Joshua Vivuer ran with ze script in hand and belted through ze door he had left a long time ago. For, you see, ze first time I had seen him, he had exited ze theater. Now he understood what he had to do to free the apparitions. I reminded him, and now he was setting his future in stone. I had achieved the bettering of my day by giving a human a push in the right direction. He was seeing ze past and ze future and couldn't make it go away. I clacked my beak, blinked my black eyes, and then moved my crow feet. I had made ze future. Without the boost of confidence I had tricked him into, he would never have been able to beg the theater using his persuasion. Ze only way I knew zis was because I knew ze future. I was ze time ark. And ze apparitions had been real. I had brought zem back using zis time-traveling power I have. I zen told zem what to say, and told zem ze unbelievable, fantastical truth about me. Zat script however, would someday become a staple of entertainment. He would try again to send it in. And it, in turn, would be rejected again till ze theater finally accepted it, and deemed it ze finest script to ever have been written. I would visit him again and give him some more of my time-ark-act to help him along. But for now zis would suffice. Zis entertainment had only started today. And it would take many more years for my miserable day to really end. Ze best zing about zis was zat I knew what I was waiting for. It spoiled ze surprise. Nonetheless, it was a good one. One I could barely wait for. And what would happen with ze script was zat it would inspire a series of plays. Zen it would create moving pictures. A series of moving pictures. It would also create book series' and become its very own genre. My only regret is zat I don't have enough power to bring anyone along for zis ride I will experience. I am alone. And I am ze oldest crow in ze history of time. Ze only time I don't feel zis loneliness is when I watch Vivuer go out into his day-to-day ways. Like when I taught Joshua to not give up with ze script by baiting him with fiction. I, ze French crow, made him ze greatest playwright ze world had ever seen, besides Shakespeare of course.

000000000IIIII200IIIII200IIIII20000IIIII000002IIIIIIIII000002IIIIIIIII:

A BLOB OF GREY
BY AMBER UNGER

"Hi! My name's Orange. And I'm here to tell you a story. Let me start from the beginning. Well, ish. You'll hear about how I got my name later. For now, let's just skip that part. One day, I was peacefully waddling about (I have short legs), when I found myself on top of a rather strange and tall object. Strange to me because I hadn't truly noticed it before now. Its surface was smooth, vast, and, need I say, flat. It had four wooden legs that kept the top above the floor. I looked down toward the ground, which was very far away from me now that I had subconsciously climbed the leg of this, this, thing. I looked up and down, observing every little detail that I had never seen before. Waddling about the ground never really let me see the true image of this place. But now that I had discovered this area, I was able to look out of the transparent quadrilateral and see what magnificent scenery lay beyond it. How I longed to explore the vast extension of the world. I couldn't fulfill this dream right now, as I was stuck in a house. Someday, though. Someday, I would escape from this giant's den. In the future, I would discover lands far from this one. Or would I? Sorry, I just *adore* adding little narrator bits. He he! Anyway, back to the story. I waddled over to the scenic portal (I called it that because I didn't know what it was at the time), and pressed my face against it, admiring the nature I so loved at that moment. The sky was a bright blue that complimented the soft, green grass surrounding tall trees and hills. Suddenly, an idea popped in my head. I would go to the room where the tall, solid rectangle was and somehow get out. So off I wobbled. It took a little long to get there since I was so small and slow, but at least I made it. Once, when I was slightly younger, I fell over while trying to get to my bed and couldn't get up for a few minutes. It was awful. But that's part of a different story. At the rectangle, I reached up for the sphere coming out of it. I couldn't reach it by a long shot, so I tried a different approach. While pacing around, trying to think of a way out, I stepped on a push pin, which I called pointy-sharp thing at the moment. Thinking it was a sharp-enough tool for my escape, I used it to poke a hole in a soft spot, in the adjacent wall to the door. I continued by poking more holes and several pokes later, I connected the holes and cut an outline for the smaller door. Once finished, I plopped down on the floor. I wasn't used to labor, nor was I ready to get used to it. Now, I could have easily just walked out of that doorway and into freedom, but being the unintelligent blob I was, I first built a door to fit the unfinished gap. After resting again, I slowly crept out the door, not sure whether it was safe or not. The sunlight tickled my translucent-grey skin. It felt unusual, soothing, and I did not want to leave my current spot. I knew what I had to do, though. I had had the mission ever since I was born. I was to go to the mountain. I knew which mountain, only I didn't know why. After dismissing the thought, I started my journey at full speed. I ran and ran. My running didn't last long, however, due to my lack of athleticism. I was out of breath and panting, but it was worth it because I could no longer see any of my former surroundings. I got over my heavy breathing and then ran some more, as even more hours passed by. By now, I was already a quarter around the planet without even noticing. The run so far had been more than good and even refreshing compared to the dirty-aired house. The rest of the journey however, was *horrible.* Obstacle after obstacle stopped it from going any quicker. And at the size I was, everything was three times the challenge. At one point, I came upon an ocean which I had to swim across to get to my next stop. As if that wasn't enough, I also had to get past a mob of crazy children who thought I was adorable and wanted to keep me as a pet. They petted and prodded. And worst of all, they *held* me! Mm kay! Time for a drink of water! All of this story-telling is making me thirsty! (One cup of water later...) Just a second now; wait till I'm done... clearing my throat... Let us start the story. So I went on, every now and then stopping to ward off some stray beast. The nights were bitter, the days hot, but I made it through. Now it's time to tell the scary part. Well, it was difficult, not really that scary though.... Anyway, about 1 hour, 37 minutes, 15 seconds, and 12 milliseconds after the children, I ran into a group of muggers. Who, when they discovered I had *literally* nothing on me, also thought I was cute and wanted to bring me home. It wasn't long until I was captured by a mad scientist who wanted to conduct absurd experiments with me. I mean, on. Okay! Time to tell you how I got my name. I was born as an orange in the very house I had just barely escaped from. Then I grew up and turned into a two-foot-tall, short-armed, short-legged, translucent, light-grey creature. I guess I should get back now. As the mad scientist was preparing the ingredients for an experiment to specify my species, I slithered through the too-loose straps which kept me somewhat snug on the experimental chair. I was running around the vertical pole below the chair while holding onto it, when I was interrupted by Mr. M.S., who had recently noticed my escape. I began scurrying around the room with my arms in the air, screaming like a little girl, and the scientist eventually fell for my little kid act. In his sulking despair, I was able to successfully creep out the door. After that traumatic experience, I was famished! So I stopped by Subway to order a sub. While I was there, I briefly met a young girl standing with her father in the front of the line. I was waiting to order, when her balloon suddenly popped. She turned around, pointed her skinny finger at me, and angrily yelled, '*he* did it!' in a shrill, irritating voice.

I gulped nervously as her father turned around with a furious face. I hadn't developed the skill of speaking to this species yet, which meant I had no way of defending myself. The incredibly strong man picked me up with fury. Then, as if he had been lifting twenty-eight pound weights for three years straight, threw me down. I felt a bit dizzy, but in the end, I had gotten my foot-long Sub I had ordered. *What*, I was starved! I caught a bus to the next city, and then carried on my adventure on foot once again. It soon ended when I met my old friend, Mr. M. Scientist, at a marathon. I was rooting for number thirteen, who ran at a similar pace as me. (That was why I was rooting for her.) And apparently at some point, the scientist had put a tracker on me which was why it was so easy to escape earlier. I concentrated on the marathon again as number thirteen was just about to touch the finish line and come in fifth. Suddenly, Mr. M.S. grabbed me by the arm. "Oh! I didn't know *you* were into dancing!"

I gushed while batting my non-existent eyelashes, beginning to move into step with the flustered being.

An angry Mad Scientist wriggled out of my grasp, and then smiled a wide, evil grin. "Let's race," he replied.

"Hmm, depends on the reason."

Mad Scientist slapped his head in annoyance, "Ugh. Fine. I'll tell you. To observe your physical abilities, etc., etc."

"Good enough for me!"

I followed him down the stadium to the now-empty track. We raced for thirty-two minutes, both being incredibly slow and unable to reach the finish line. By the end, the race finished quickly; one hour and forty-seven minutes, and in a tie. We were so tired that we didn't bother with a tie-breaker. Instead, we glared each other down one last time, and then left in search of a thirst quencher. Soon after, I was at my second last pit stop. There, I found a small village that was five miles away from my destination, the mountain. It was here that I met two neighboring and friendly folk, claiming to be "Yellow" and "Purple Dot." I explained that I was Orange, and surprise struck both of their faces.

"You've got to be kidding me, mate!" Dot exclaimed in his pure Australian accent. Actually, now that I think about it, he had a *Russian accent.* Wait, no, he was *Polish!* Mmm, nope, Ukranian? Hmm, Arabian? Celtic? Italian? Oh! Ah! *Now* I remember! American! Yep, that's it! And the other one was, British. They gathered nourishments for the rest of the trip and then dragged me off in the direction of the mountain. It was only now that I started pondering over *why* I needed to get there. The thought nagged me and nagged me until I finally gathered up the courage to ask Yellow and Purple Dot.

The only answer I got was merely, "I know as much as you do, but a *little* more," they answered in sync.

"We're almost there, though," Yellow assured us afterward. The travelling was *much* easier now that we were relieved of the fact that there could be miles ahead of us, but there wasn't. Phew! Our relief, however, was short-lived as the scientist was standing right in front of us.

"Um, do you know this guy?" Purple asked. I gulped.

"Unfortunately, yes, I do," I answered regretfully.

"Oh, I haven't come to party; I came to stop you from getting the prize," his voice sounded creepy and a little higher than usual.

"Huh?" Yellow questioned.

"I *said*-"

"We *heard* what you said, but what do you mean by *prize*?" Purple asked.

"Why, the three miniature rodents don't even know why they're here, or what they're here for. Ha! Pathetic creatures! Oh, will you look at the time. I've gotta go. Toodle-oo!"

He jogged about a meter ahead of us and then came back to handcuff us together. His mistake, however, was that *I* don't *have* hands. And Yellow had neither hands nor arms. I slipped out of the stylish yet useful bracelets. Then, I freed Purple Dot with the scientist's key, which I stole while he was handcuffing us, and the three of us sprinted toward the half-a-mile away mountain. On our way there, we ran out of food and got distracted by the many fruit-bearing plants. We stuffed our mouths and packs with the fruits, leaving no room for whatever was in that mountain. The Scientist was already there, enjoying what waited for us. When we finally arrived, we found him in a cave, snacking on a holographic chocolate bar that he apparently thought was real. The hologram was being produced by a silver, flat circle that was finished off with a yellow light in the very center. The scientist was also ready to board a holographic airplane which would take him to wherever he desired. We watched in silence, allowing giggles and chuckles to rip through the air. M.S. sharply turned around to face us with a disgusted look. "How did you pesky rascals escape? No, never mind that; why are you giggling? Actually, no, it doesn't matter because you'll never be seeing me again!"

I slapped my forehead at the Scientist's ignorance. He, of course, thought that the plane was also real.

Just then, I realized something. "Hold on; if what we were looking for was a hologram the whole time, then why was our quest to come here?"

Suddenly, the hologram switched from the extremely convincing plane to a plump, short female who looked significantly a lot like, well, me. Only *she* wasn't translucent. Instead, she had blindingly beautiful, orange skin. As we were staring at the speaking figure, the scientist realized the dream transportation was no longer there, *and* that it was really a hologram. Anger flew out of the temperamental man as he stomped towards the four of us.

But the mysterious lady's eyes said it all. "Stop."

A firm voice commanded in my head. Every living creature in, on, or by the mountain, even the plants, froze.

"Oh, stop the silly tricks, you, you … just wait a minute. I'm trying to think what to call her. Ah! You, you, ghost!" Mad Scientist sputtered. As you can see, the freezing didn't work on him for long.

"I am no ghost, and this is not just a holographic projector, it's a transporter.'

As the confuzzled human reached out to touch her, she was as solid as any other object surrounding us. This was quite the surprise to everyone in the cave.

"But, but how?!" The Scientist didn't know what to believe anymore. He was surrounded by madness. Besides himself, of course.

"But how, indeed, Gregory Frérot?" His eyebrows rose up. His body shook, his knees wobbled, and his mouth slowly dropped open.

"My name, how… How do you know?"

"Oh, I'm friends with your mother on Facebook!"

"Anyway," Yellow butted in. "I thought you were going to tell us why we were supposed to come here?" she asked as Gregory toyed furiously with the holographic projector on the ground. Finally finding the right button for the transporter, he simply vanished with the device.

"Heh, I was planning on telling you my name first," she replied, chuckling. The cave became eerily silent. "Neutrice."

"Hmm?" I questioned.

"Neutrice. My name is Neutrice."

"Oh, and the purpose of this task?" I asked.

"My son, I have brought you here to find light in the dark times. To find a solution to your problems. To tell you, never give up, no matter how hard and how dark things seem. And to fight a great battle against Gregory here."

By then, Greg had already teleported to the summit of the mountain which we were in.

"Wait. You're my mama?!" I shouted with confusion.

"You're his mama?!" Yellow and Purps repeated.

"Mm hmm. And proud to be it," her voice began breaking up as tears welled up in her eyes. Giving my mother a tight hug, I explained how I was proud to be her son.

"Go fight your fight, Orange."

"I will, mom." With that, we three friends started climbing up the rest of the mountain. Once at the top, we found the Mad Scientist, Gregory Frérot, wearing boxing gloves. "Oh, that's not the type of fight *I* want, Gregory." I said right before pulling out a gun. Little did Frérot know that the gun didn't shoot bullets. Instead, out popped a flag which said, bang! This frightened Frérot so much that he backed right off of the mountain and into our elaborate trap. The original plan was to dump him off at the nearest prison. But that was before we realized that the house I originally lived in or was trapped in was directly beside the mountains. I felt truly ashamed for going all the way around the world when I could have easily just walked seventeen steps and up the stony hill. That's besides the matter, though. Purple came up with the idea to lock the doctor of science in that exact house since *I* wouldn't be living there anymore. After we finished with him, we returned to the cave where my mother was.

"Um, Mom?"

"Yes?" she answered.

"How did I—we, find light?"

"What a great question that is, Orange. The way *you* found light was by making new friends. You didn't quite know it, but you were lonely in that house. That's why you wanted to go to the mountain. You remembered what I said to you when you were but a baby. If you ever feel lonely, think about me and then you'll remember this and my message. Go to the mountain that overlooks the house. You'll know what that means when you're older. *And now* you're right where I wanted you to be—in my arms."

Okay! So that was the story! Comment down below and don't forget to like and subscribe! Bye! Tune in next time for a more accurate version of the story! (P.S.: I'm not actually going to post the more accurate story on my channel.)

000000000IIIII2000000000:

PATTHAR AND THE QUEST FOR KHAJAANA

Long ago, on the western side of Punjab, there lived a man named Boldar with his wife, Chattaan. Now, Boldar was a poor man who scrounged the outreaches of India for whatever occupation he could find to earn him a few rupees. But, of course, every day at the end of his work, he was left with a small amount. India had its fair share of poverty and it never got better. Then one day, Boldar came home, through the jungle of screeching monkeys and past the marketplace of merchants.

"I'm home!" he announced with weariness. The only reply he got was sobbing from the small space that served as a living room. He closed the door behind him and took off his sandals before walking into the kitchen and out into a decorated room. "What is the matter, my Chattan?" He investigated the reason for her weeping.

"You know exactly what, husband! We have no money for food and the kachori that I sell in the marketplace earns very little. We cannot survive like this for long. And what about little Patthar? It'll be hard not to pickpocket from the rich."

"You know that I won't let that happen. I'll ask my greedy, good for nothing brother to lend me a tiny bit of money."

"And what if he says no again, Boldar? What if he curses at us for not being rich like the rest of your family? What if he screams at you to leave because you're nothing but a peasant? There has to be some other way to keep our lives from falling to pieces."

"There isn't, Chattan," he placed a hand on her cheek and in a whisper continued, "there is no other way." At that very moment, the door was thrust open.

"I'm home, mama and papa!" twelve-year-old Patthar yelled. The conversation between the two adults instantly ceased and the mother went to the doorway of the kitchen.

"How was school, little Patthar?"

"Oh, it was fine, mama. But Jaffar called me a Carabí Itha."

"Don't listen to him, son. He's just a big bully," Chattan said reassuringly. The father passed the figure in the doorway and arrived at a counter top by the light-brown and dark-haired boy. From an alcove in the wall, he procured a mango. Taking a big bite of it, he pretended no one else was in his vicinity.

"What's the matter, Father?"

"What?" Boldar turned his head to his son.

"You have one of those something-is-wrong looks on your face."

"I," he stammered before looking to his thin-framed wife. Patthar's father himself had a skinny form, a wispy greying beard amongst black, and blue eyes that whispered of the Bay of Bengal. Chattan replied with a furious shake of her covered head and a silencing glare that Boldar ignored.

"My Patthar, your mother and I have been discussing the possibility of a vacation."

"Oh! Are we going to 'Imagicaa,' Father?"

"No," he hesitated, "We're not going to an amusement park, son. Besides, it's miles away from here, all the way in Khopoli, Maharashtra. The city that is too far away, Patthar. And you know that we don't have a money tree. It is much too expensive. No, we're going to your uncle's mansion in Ludhiana."

"What if I don't want to, Papa?"

"You have no choice, Patthar; there is nowhere else to go."

"But, Papa, Uncle is a terrible man," Patthar complained.

"He's not bad, Son, just a little misguided."

"Well, I don't want to go! I know why you're going to Uncle's, Papa. We're poor people," the boy happily grinned from ear to ear.

"We're not poor people," Boldar reassured, "but we're also not rich."

"Well, I don't care! I'm gonna find a way so we don't have to go to Uncle's place. Maybe I'll find us a money tree. We're going to be the richest family in Punjab," Patthar's rucksack left his shoulders and plopped down on the ground. The tin door was pushed open, letting the skinny, famished boy to flee from the little-brown hut that stood on the outskirts of Ludhianna. Chattan yelled a protest and would've gone after her son if her husband hadn't been there to stop her.

"Don't worry, my Chattan. He'll be back; just wait. In a few days, he'll come home like the prodigal son," Boldar attempted to calm his wife, only to achieve a curious glare.

"How can you be so sure? Life is dangerous beyond our hut, beyond the outskirts. He won't come back! Just you see! And where's he going to go?"

Boldar had a twinkle in his eye and smiled a mysterious apparition of a smile. "I might've given him some of Daddy B's knowledge. Whilst we spoke, you didn't notice me step closer to him, did you?"

"No," she stated worriedly and with a hint of a smile. "You didn't."

"I did," he said with a mischievous look about him.

Patthar looked wildly around at everything he would leave behind, which in reality was only a two-bedroom hut made of dirt, straw, and mud. But he would also be leaving behind the string of nicer huts that surrounded his. They lived poorly in a place where only rich people lived. Their house was an ugly duckling. And the thought of making his parents happy with his return with what he imagined to be treasure, was so great it drowned the emptiness in his stomach. Returning home with the promise of poverty ending would end his mama and papa's arguments that often strayed to leaving India forever. It had been talked about before between Chattan and Boldar how life would be easier if they moved to a new country. To leave their native land and go where Chattan's mama and papa were. Canada. He knew that the only way he could make his parents rich was by finding treasure. And treasure in his eyes meant lots of gold rupees, and gems of every colour. The question was… where would he find such a thing? In the century-old legend he was familiar with, a young man found treasure but also discovered an object that held an ancient being. A being that held power and more treasure than anyone could ever imagine. No matter how much that reality tempted the boy's mind, it was too much for him, even though a part of him denied that it wasn't. The boy had been trailing in a deep cloud of thought and when he looked up, he saw that the hut was gone. He had wandered subconsciously to the thought of finding a cave in the middle of nowhere. All that surrounded him was sand. And for a long time all he knew was the fine material that littered his side of the world as he wandered like the lost child he was. Mother and Father would have been disappointed although his father would be the most at hearing of his son's loss of knowing his surroundings. For two whole days, Patthar wandered the desert and finally came to a village. He had just barely survived off of spiny-tailed lizards and small oasis that signified that Lady Varuna was with him. The young boy would soon learn from an elder of the village that the village was called Gannv (Gow). While there, the boy asked for food and water. And in return, the elder, Bazuraga, questioned Patthar. The two sat on cushions placed on the ground of the elder's tent. He wanted to know the reason for the young wanderer's aimless journey in the desert. He was answered with the truth. The wanderer had gotten lost looking for riches. All Bazuraga did was scoff at the young adventurer, "Leave at once, you scoundrel! You should've never come back." He stood tall with a complete mane of white hair billowing in the wind that blew from the open flap of the tent.

"What you mean? Who left?" Patthar stood up as well but with a confusion that battled against the old man's serious expression. The man then swiftly plucked a hidden katara from a sheath on the ground. A katara is an Indian dagger commonly used for religious ceremonies.

"You know exactly who, Patthar, you liar! Your people, they stole my daughter and my cow, just because I didn't want to give up what they wanted. I have already suffered because of the dayan. Because of the witch that switched their souls around, cursing them forever."

"But who were they, Bazuraga? Do you know who they were?" Patthar pushed the latter statement into the back of his mind.

"Stop playing this game. You know who they were! It was Mara and his group of bandits. And they left you behind, didn't they?" the suspicious man firmly held his anger.

"For the last time, no! I come from a poor family. We live somewhere over there," he pointed to where he supposed he lived. "I was in the desert looking for some way to stop my parents grumbling about being poor. I want to be like everyone else in my neighborhood, on the outskirts." The elder grew quiet and let the dagger fall to the ground with a thud.

"I don't know if to trust what you say, little one. But I'll give you a chance," the elder went to retrieve something from a wooden chest in the corner of the ornately trimmed tent. He came back with a glass vial that held a clear liquid too perfect to be water. "The bandits, two moons ago, wanted to know where to find a magical scimitar. At first, I resisted telling but I had no choice. I had to stop them from taking away my family. It, of course, was a useless attempt. The legend says that the magical scimitar of Akbar is buried in a cave. A cave that can be found by Eagle's Peak. If you drink this it'll give you the ability to fly and the small mountain where the cave is… should be very easy to find," saying so, Bazuraga handed the vial to Patthar.

"You want me to rescue your cow and daughter?"

"Yes, Patthar. If you are part of the bandits, they will see you and kill you for coming back to me and my village. But if you have nothing to do with them, you can steal back what's mine. Of course, you might be a bandit either way, and it doesn't really matter who you are because they'll try to kill you no matter what. Personally though, I don't think you are, Patthar," the wise old man slyly winked.

"How can I trust you? How do I know this isn't poison?" the boy asked, nodding toward the vial.

"Would I poison you, young one?" Bazuraga became serious.

Without hesitating, the young adventurer answered, "Probably, yes. But I don't think you did," the boy grinned. He tilted back his head with a push of the thumb, flicking the cork open. With one gulp, a quarter of the liquid disappeared down his throat. Bazuraga nodded a confirmation on how much should be swallowed and he lowered his head before closing the vial, giving it back to the elder. He took it and went to go place it back in the chest. Patthar, on the other hand, was already feeling what he presumed was the enchanted potion. A light fizzing in his stomach erupted that eventually moved to his upper back as something pushed through. The wise elder came back to Patthar.

"Go find them, Patthar, before nightfall! The flying spell takes you exactly where you wish to go. So all you have to do to get to your destination is to think of Eagle's Peak. You do know where that is?"

"Yes, yes, I do," he confirmed as he left the tent. Once out, he smiled and waved at the giant crowd of villagers who had sprung up from their very own tents. They waved back and the boy turned to do what any flier does, lift off. From out of the corner of his eye, he noticed a shimmering of white on his back. He had grown a pair of wings that were neither short nor long. A pair of wings that were a glossy, angelic-gray. The boy gulped;' today was a dream to him. With a run, he jumped into the sky, only to fall back down. He tried it once more and this time he found that the wind was gracious. Little Patthar soared through the sky. Along the way, he decided that if he wasn't actually in control of the wings, he could just put his hands away from the tiring stance that held in the air. So that's what he did. He put his hands in his trouser pockets, and lo-and-behold, he found a piece of paper. A note. His father had been his sneaky self again. But what he didn't understand was when it was given to him. He shrugged it off.

It read,

"Dear Patthar, by the time you've gotten this you're probably wondering how it got to be in your pocket. A short story even shorter, I knew that you would go looking for treasure since your mother and I argue about our wealth ninety percent of the time. So I had this great idea to write you a note so you would know exactly where to find it. Anyway, many years ago when I was your age, I found an old map in a chest my father owned. I kept it, believing it would make me rich. However when I got older, I started treating it like a fairytale. I didn't think it was real and we needed the money. So I sold it to a trader in Ludhiana. Ever since then, I've regretted selling it and to this day, I believe it was a real map leading to riches. P.S: you can find the trader Bauba and his shop, Bauba's Black

Market on Brown Road Street. It should be real easy to find, and anyway, good luck, my Patthar. Yours truly, Father."

The young adventurer stuffed the note back in his pocket, turning it word for word in his thoughts. What the bandits were looking for wasn't his quest. Wherever that map led, that was his quest. A quest to make his papa and mama proud of their only son. The only problem was he didn't have any rupees. And rupees to him was the money he could use to buy back the map. But for now all he could do was fly on and think about what waited for him at Eagle's Peak. Once a day had passed of this one-way journey, he gently started descending. The magic of the angelic wings had a mind of its own and so it dropped him behind the safety of a tall rock. The wings popped into nothingness and the traveler was left gazing from behind the rock. Five tents had been set up alongside five large camels, and a sand covered cow was tied to one of the five tents. In front of all this and a couple meters away was a rise of rock that led to a gaping hole in the mountain. The dark cloak of one of the bandits was seen disappearing down it. The coast was now clear. And with a sneaky jog, Patthar started searching each tent for the missing daughter. After searching four of the five zig-zagging tents, he came to the last and farthest one. Parting the sides of the tent's entrance, he found who he was looking for. There, tied to a large, wooden rod that kept the tent standing, was a *ghoonghat*-covered teenager who was presumed to be Bazuraga's only daughter. She beamed with relief.

"I was sent by your father to rescue you and your cow," the hero of the story announced to the rescued. Of course, all he received was a moo and then he remembered what the elder had said about the witch, and the curse. Attempting to untie the rope that constrained her; he noticed a shining object hidden behind a velvet curtain on the far wall. Pulling himself up, he gravitated toward the curtain, and pushing it aside, he found exactly what he needed. He took it without a hesitant look and clutched the gold-hilted Katara with a promise to never let go. Back by the prisoner, he took the harsh material in one hand and with a few cuts; the thick rope was in chunks. The knife was then secured to his billowing harem trousers by way of tying a thin piece of the curtain onto a small slit he had made with the sharp blade. He had quickly gone over to the curtain after cutting the hostage free and cut a strip off. The daughter stood up and Patthar motioned for her to follow him, leading them behind the jutting stone where he had hid before. A few more cow sounds were used while they exited the tent and then the boy adventurer placed the rescued on the back of the cow.

"Wait here," he gently commanded as he lowered his face to the cow's. "What do I call you?" The cow stared at him with an unblinking gaze.

"Rajakumari. But Rajak will do," she whispered before going back to being silent. Patthar nodded and then stood up, walking briskly to the cave that had been burrowed into the mountain. Little Patthar was a little older now. His birthday had been yesterday, and before that had been the day that he had started his quest. But now, he had a little plan of his own. He needed Rupees, and this enchanted weapon could give him that. Boldar's heir stepped foot into the dark and moist cave. Treading carefully, he heard an echo from a distance. The cave curved to the right and light was dimmed as it went deeper into the earth. He was close now; he could hear the bandits working. They were digging rock out. Looking for something. Time ticked by and light had ceased into dark before coming back once again. Patthar hid behind a ridge, and looked down into a lower level. This floor had broken through into a small room where a tunnel led to an unseen area where the bandits worked. Apart from all that, a dim light glowed from within the tunnel. The clamoring of tools ended and then silence took over before someone from within shouted with victory.

"Hurrah, Mara! We've found the burial chamber of Akbar! You were right! It's here!"

Another man spoke. "First, Dukhadai, let us have a break of a fresh drink of water and some chole. I am starving, and trust me, a working man must eat. Especially before becoming very rich. Do you agree, boss?"

"Sure, sure, Bhukha Adami!" Footsteps sounded as the treasure hunters came closer and closer to exiting the tunnel. Five men stepped out of their hiding place. The tallest and skinniest of the five wore an eyepatch over his left eye, and a scar peeked out from under the patch, this one had only a moustache. The next three wore turbans, each having a different sized beard, and each having kirpans at their sides. The only real difference between these three bandits was their chiseled faces, the colourful trousers, and the vests. Which left the last one to be a large man who was bald and had not a beard, only a few hairs of a stubble chin. One by one, the five bandits climbed up the wooden ladder that was propped against the side of the large hole. It was close to where Patthar was now hunched. That changed as they came closer to his hiding spot. He stepped back further into the shadows. The group of burly figures passed by and the hiding intruder waited till they were long gone before quickly climbing down into the room. Patthar then entered the tunnel that had been used to dig. It led into a larger room that owned a primitive casket made of dried mud. But what interested the quester was the bronze chest at the far end of the burial chamber. His heavily decorated surroundings and the displacement of armor, which the boy recognized as the varying costume of the Rajput, was nothing compared to the large box. The Rajput had been warriors long ago that had protected India from its enemies and invaders such as the Delhi Sultans, and the Mughals. Past the coffin, he bent down over the chest. No key was needed to open the lock as the lid was lifted. Inside the container was a lining of scarlet cushioning that supported a small package in a light-brown covering. Exposing the item underneath the thin wrapping, Patthar glanced down with a smirk. The rugged hilt of a scimitar was looking back at him. No blade was visible, but he had heard enough of the legends to know that only the sun or a powerful source of light could reveal the rest of the weapon. The bandits would be back any time now. The adventurer had an idea. The dagger from before was taken and placed into the wrapping while the priceless scimitar took the dagger's position in the trouser rip. He concealed the fake artifact, the chest was closed, and then Patthar left the chamber as quickly as he could. He pulled himself up the ladder and then hid in the opposite wall of the one he had been hiding behind before. As soon as he took coverage behind the wall, the group of robbers walked swiftly by. And the leader, Mara, was in a fluster. "Someone was here! They took my dagger, the cow, and the girl we stole from that stupid village."

"We'll get the beetle who did this. If anything, he's down there taking what's ours."

Mara nodded as he calmed down and then the group of four went down into the tunnel. The small figure crept out of hiding and ran slowly in the other direction. A howling was heard from the burial chamber as Patthar ran out of the cave. He was gonna go to the concealed cow and daughter, and from what he assumed, they hadn't been found. That meant that he was very close to stealing from those who stole. Patthar was about to walk further away from the cave when he heard the swish of a sword being pulled out and a snarl of a voice.

"Going somewhere, boy?"

Patthar turned around, and there standing in front of him was the fifth bandit. He had failed to realize that these men had set a trap for him. He gulped. "I asked, boy, going somewhere?"

The criminal waved his sword around, threatening to harm his victim. Instead of answering, Patthar fumbled at his belt for the dagger. Remembering that he had traded it for the hilt, he drew that instead, hoping that the legends were true. Muttering a final prayer under his breath, he turned around to fight. But it stayed still, no change.

"You gonna fight me, boy? With a stolen weapon? What a foolish boy you are! See, it doesn't even work. But since you want to fight, might as well get rid of a future pain in the back."

The bandit advanced and swung his blade at the young adversary's neck. With an alarming jolt from the faulty hilt in the boy's hands, it grew. A sharp, curving blade slid out and the enemy's own blade struck the shiny metal, and bounced back. Patthar's opponent swore in surprise and picked his fallen sword from the sand. He then lunged at the intruder and brought his sword down against the other. As it collided with the dark-yellow blade, something happened. The underling of the two broke in shards and the man belonging to Mara's gang of treasure hunters, was infuriated. Nothing was sprung from this, for a meaty hand was clamped upon his shoulder.

"I see we've captured our thief." The trapped individual looked up, realizing he had been caught. The one-eyed man stood there with one of three bearded henchmen.

"Be careful; he's got what's rightfully ours," the henchman with the broken sword warned.

"Don't need to warn me, [8]Cetavani," Mara moved closer to their guest. "Where did you put my treasures?"

No answer.

"Give it to me," he pointed to the scimitar.

Instead, Patthar pulled it farther back from the demanding man.

"Why should I? Why should I give it to the robber of graves?"

The villain he was, only sneered further at the boy and it was at this time that the young one looked around to discover that they weren't alone. The ensemble of crooks surrounded them and now backed off. Patthar had a bad feeling about this and it only got worse when the man in the black eyepatch drew his scimitar.

"You leave me no choice but to kill you in a duel. You'll regret taking my things and not telling me where you hid them. You should've given me the artifact, but no. Prepare to die!" The duel commenced without further intervention and with a swipe of the bronze scimitar in Mara's hand, the golden blade furthered upward to achieve a clashing rhythm. They parried each other's blows, until with surprise the weakest scimitar of the two didn't break with two strokes. Instead, it fared rather well beside the point in which Mara was left unparried and pressed the winning scimitar to his opponent's neck. Patthar gasped as the circle of laughing men closed in and snatched the blade from his very hands.

"Not so mighty now," the bandits taunted him. A dark-grin grew on the one-eyed man's lips as he took the weapon. For as the

8 Che-Tav-nee

leader of the bandits touched it, the spell faded away and the hilt was just exactly that. A handle with no sharp end.

"It's got a mind of its own, I guess!" Patthar smirked as he pushed to his knees against the rough sand. The powdery substance sneaked up his trouser legs, rubbing painfully against his skin.

"Hehe, I guess so," the bandit who pretended to be a pirate, slapped Patthar across the right cheek after faking a laugh. "You know, boy, I don't care about this thing."

The hilt was then passed around the group of bandits but no change occurred. It was then given back to the previous holder, and it instantaneously changed into the long blade it had been. Being taken back furtively, it was placed in the hands of one of the unnamed bandits.

"I have found a new interest," the villainous, brown-skinned grave robber stated. A long digit on his left hand pointed to the prisoner's chest. "You!"

"Why? What use am I to you?"

"I could sell you, boy! Or if you are of a rich family line, I could ransom you."

The prisoner wrestled against the arms that held him. "My family is more than rich. My father, he's Tipu the Great. And if he hears of this, he's gonna kill you all and leave you to die in the desert. To be picked clean by the vultures."

"Is that right, boy?" he leaned in.

"Stop calling me boy; I have a name!"

"What's your name then, prince?" a smile was evident on the questioner's face.

Patthar was hesitant, "Jahangir. My name's Jahangir!"

"You hear that, brothers? His name's Jahangir," the bandits chortled in laughter. Mara leaned again. "You lie! I've met the king's son, and he's as fat as an ox."

"I've lost weight," the fake prince protested. He was ignored as a gentle push from the one-eyed Indian sent him onto the sand.

"Tie him up, Cetavani! By the state of his ragged clothes he's surely not a prince. He's looking for what we seek. Khajaana! And it's all for his family. For Boldar and Chattan."

The Sikh with the longest beard bent down with a bundle of rope. It was the same, coarse type of rope that had been used to tie up the princess. The bandits stopped.

"How do you know my parents?"

The skinny headman was suddenly sullen, and he stared reminiscently at Patthar. Then with a flick of a button, an alarmed but curious expression befell him.

"So you are their son," he grew quiet.

"You still want me to tie him up?" asked the short-bearded Sikh, Cetavani.

"Yes. We'll bring him to Salevara, and then we leave him alone. He should've never come here. It's all his fault for what happens next. Finish tying him up, Cetavani. Then bring him to my tent. We're leaving very soon, before nightfall."

"Why can't I watch him?" the tallest of the Sikhs whined.

"No, Lamba, you come with me."

"Then, at least tell me. What are you going to do with the artifact?" asked an interested Lamba after being rejected by his leader.

Mara stopped walking away and glanced back. He then took the artifact out of hiding.

“Here, have it! Don’t at any costs let him get his hands on it!”

Throwing the hilt to the sandy ground, Lamba thrust it into his vest. The others left the chosen and shortest of the five to tend to the boy. It was the guy who had trapped Patthar in the first place. And now he had a chance to exact a sort of revenge for embarrassing him at his scimitar fighting. He held the roll of rope tightly in his hands and got to his knees as he started to tie up the prisoner. The young quester thought up a quick plan of action while wondering what the true identity of the man who knew his parents was. He looked up at the sand that he was lying on and noticed something close to his head. With one of his hands free and with a hope that harm would be only to the extent of unconsciousness, he grabbed the large, smooth rock. Then, with what little strength he had, he hurled the rock. He looked back at the sand and then when the thud of victory sounded, he slowly sneaked a look behind him. There, lying on the sand was the man who was supposed to tie him up.

Getting up quickly, Patthar started to search through his captor’s coat. He reclaimed what was his and took off at a sprint, never stopping to look back. Then, dropping to a lower level, he headed for his hiding place. The first part of his quest was almost complete.

He delved behind the cliff wall to the waiting daughter and her pet.

“Sorry for a long wait,” he apologized.

“All is well, but we must be going before the bad men come back to discover that you’ve escaped,” the cow took the apology with the princess’s voice.

“A cow and a princess’s mind put in each other is very weird. You saw what happened by the cave entrance?” Patthar sounded surprised.

"Of course, I did. I couldn't just sit here doing nothing."

He nodded as he leapt onto the cow's back, resulting in Rajakumari, the princess, protesting with a moo. Soon, the three were heading in the direction that Patthar had come from. It was a couple of minutes after they had departed from the cliff side when the leader of the bandits got suspicious over the fact that Cetavani hadn't returned yet. He exited his tent, automatically bringing his other henchman at his side. Looking to where the cave entrance was to the north, his eyes widened and he ran to the ledge right of it. The others followed close behind to see what their leader had seen.

"You idiot! You let him get away!" The unconscious man awakened with a start, realizing at once what had happened.

"I'm sorry, Mara. I didn't mean to."

"Of course you didn't. But you failed and now you must walk when we start to travel. No camel to aid you; only your own feet."

"Are we going to chase after him?" Dukhadai questioned. The leader of the bandits shook his head and picked up a small piece of paper. Opening it up, he grinned maliciously.

"I think that there's a shortcut *per se*. We're gonna meet him at this Bauba's Black Market," he cackled with laughter as the note went around, sending more laughter into the air. Patthar wasn't done with the group of bandits, as he had thought.

The travel back to the village felt quicker than the travel to. The strange part about arriving back in Gannv (Gow) was that as soon as he had passed the first tent, something changed. It turned into a stone hut, bordering against a gate while it gave birth to a long wall that kept the village in a squareish pen. Patthar figured that the village elder hadn't told him everything. The witch who had cursed his daughter, had also cursed his people and the place where he lived. Bazuraga must have been king and this village must have been a kingdom all along. The young adventurer would soon find this out by passage through the village. He first looked into the newly transformed hut that had once been a tent, but found it empty. Then, walking down the last section of the pathway that cut through the entrapment of walls, he came to the double doors of the castle. A guard stood on either side of the scarlet door with khandas hanging from their hips. Patthar began to speak, but the guards stopped him with nodding heads. The double doors opened and the boy entered through. Sliding off the smooth skin of the cow, he furthered on with it and the daughter by his side. The castle was furnished exactly how he thought it would be, ornately and positively rich. Large paintings were hung high up on the walls. Hallways of doors ran in opposite directions, giving the place a maze-like experience. Patthar passed the various furnishings that varied from cabinets and antique chairs to book shelves and wardrobes full of years of clothing.

Looking to either corridor, the three ventured down the right and carpeted one. They only took that way because it spoke more royally than the adjacent corridors. The one they had left ran further on and the left passageway that they could've gone down was inhabited by a line of citizens. Walking by another set of double doors, they stopped. Stopped as the doors split open to admit another guard.

"Welcome, Patthar! My name is [9]Sahi! I am the king's right-hand man, and I do believe that you've found his lost ones."

"Yes, I have," the boy confirmed with a nod.

9 Saw-he

Finding nothing else to say, Sahi introduced the room they were in. "Right this way. This is the throne room." The door closed behind them and the conversation continued.

"It was only when you brought the princess and the cow back that the witch's curse broke."

"See, I'm no longer a cow. I'm a princess again. A real-life princess."

"You are, Rajak, you are!" The right-hand man and Patthar looked back at the cow to see that she wasn't the one who had spoken. This time, the princess herself was indeed speaking.

"You said my shortened name, finally! Up until now all you said was Rajakumari."

She gave a small squeal. The curse on the cow and the princess had been broken. They were back to their own bodies.

And Sahi had much more to say about the witch. "This *dayan*, what was her name?" the boy asked with curiosity.

"Umm, let's see. I believe her name was Chattan. That was her name, yes—Chattan. Also, long before when King Bazuraga was but a boy, she stole a lamp from his father."

An alarmed facial expression showed on Patthar's face. The remark about the stolen lamp was nothing compared to what he had learnt about his mother. This couldn't be. His mother didn't practice magic; he was sure of it.

"You must be wrong. Chattan doesn't sound like a bad person," Patthar said, defending his mother.

"Sadly, wrong I am not, little one," they continued the walk they had halted. Now that his mother's deadly secret had been revealed, Patthar had more of a reason than ever to return home to his father. A confrontation was in order. Sahi and the trio arrived in front of a jewel-encrusted throne. Sitting rather comfortably on its cushioned seat was the same man that Patthar had seen in the tent. Except, this time the king's hair was nicely combed and clean compared to the dirty and messy hair of the village elder. His broad chin moved as conversation between Sahi and him coerced.

"The young boy as you wanted, King," the right-hand man said as he performed a small bow, which was followed by the others, who did the same.

"Good, you may leave."

The king's servant nodded and then left through the double doors of the throne room. As soon as he had left, the king got up from his throne and tearfully hugged his lost child.

"I can't believe it but at last you're back. And you are still so beautiful! Thank you so much, Patthar. Now I owe you an apology for not telling you right away who I was. But I hope I can be of some use to your quest."

"How do you know of my quest?" a puzzled Patthar asked with the simple statement of an apology never being truly acknowledged.

"Very simple. Whilst I was cursed in the shape of a peasant, I could hear the whispers of your mind. I could read what you said in invisible text. That experience, however, changed me. I now know how it feels to be poor. And I don't like it. It's utterly awful."

"I see," Patthar spoke reminiscently. Rajakumari and the unnamed cow stood, watching from one to the other. "I have been cursed by this poverty for as long as I've known. So what you just said is an encouragement to my soul."

"Then it is my pleasure, Patthar, to have you in my company."

"And I in yours, King. But I'm afraid I must be going. This search, this quest of finding a cure to poverty, must be completed as soon as I can."

"Then go, my friend! However, before you do, I must repay your kindness with a gift," the king placed a hand on Patthar's shoulder. "Two gifts that you may choose from. Take one, leave the other. Or take the other and leave the one."

"What does my gift look like, o'King?" Boldar's son curiously asked.

"Why, you know what the two choices are to be. You rescued them," a sweeping hand gestured at the daughter and the grey and white pet.

"You don't need to give me any gift, really."

"But I insist, my young friend. I must give you something to show my appreciation. Do you want my daughter for marriage? Or would you like my cow? The choice is yours, and I must say I don't care which you pick. I won't hate you for the thing you choose."

"Then it seems that I have no choice in the matter. I must pick and then leave. This search of mine can't wait."

The king gently nudged him to a tall, glass window.

"Hmph! I don't think so, Patthar. You see, us Gannvians (Gowans) have a tradition of throwing gigantic parties. As you have saved the princess from Mara and his minions, we are throwing you a party."

"But really I must be leaving, sire," the boy objected.

"Oh, no need for sire. Call me king, or, your friend. Or if you really want to, call me king, friend. But definitely not my real name, and no sires," his index finger waggled in Patthar's face to signify that the king meant business. The boy let out a sigh. There was no way out of this, no matter what. He had to participate in what his new-found friend suggested.

"I guess if I were to choose," he looked back at the daughter and the cow. "I mean, the travel to the city will be long and tiring, and a princess can't help with that. But the cow on the other hand."

"Yes?" the king suggestively interrupted.

"The cow in general isn't very reliable when going far distances, but I have no other choice."

"So, you choose the cow?" The king's face was inches away from the other's.

"Um, or should I choose the princess. No, I'm too young to marry, or am I?" The boy thought out loud with a hand on his chin and the other on his elbow.

"You're not! You're not!" the oldest of the two exclaimed with sparkling blue eyes.

"Yes, I think I know which one I'll choose," while the twelve-year-old was deciding frantically, the princess's father was whispering quietly under his breath and when a choice was made, he flung himself to the ground in despair. "I'll take the cow."

"Nooo… my foot," the king pretended as he secretly mourned for the possibility of a son-in-law. Rubbing his uninjured limb, he stood up.

"Are you okay, Father?" the princess had come up from behind, scaring him so much that he fell back down. This time, the look of agony was a little bit too real.

"I'm fine, Raj. Really I'm fine." The guest helped his host back to his feet, trying to ignore the obvious pain the other was feeling.

"Are you sure you're okay?" Patthar caringly spoke.

"Fine, fine; I'm all fine," the injured man bellowed out in painful exasperation.

"Then, I must be going," the traveler motioned for his new possession to come closer.

The injured king grabbed his arm. "No! Patthar, you must, party!" All the pain in his face suddenly left him as a large grin replaced it and the king started dancing.

Patthar turned his head to the left and stared into the camera that wasn't there. His face showed pure horror as he gulped a lungful of air. And in his head two words popped out in yellow, comical letters. *Oh no!*

The next day he got up at sunrise, took his new cow to the front gate of the castle of party goers, and said goodbye to all the new friends he had made. At a small window in the castle wall were the princess and her father. Due to the constant dancing to the merry notes of a sitar, her father looked to be in more pain than when he landed on his backside. And the loss of something precious showed in his eyes. He had been hoping that the visitor would pick the opposite of what he did. But, oh well, he still deemed his leaving guest as a wise child who would grow into an even wiser man. He looked wearisome. Which was very different from the glad and joyous expression upon the princess's complexion.

Venturing deeper and deeper into the sand-covered land, sometimes finding dry stumps of wood that never met its drink of water, Patthar thought to himself. The king of Gannv(Gow), the kingdom that Patthar now mentally called Raja had supplied his guest with a satchel of leftovers and a buffalo-skin flask containing fresh water. What would happen if he ran out of this sustenance though? That wasn't the only thought that prevailed. Now that Princess Rajakumari had left the form of the royal family's pet cow, a name for the tamed creature was needed. So to make the boring and dull trip to Ludhiana better, he thought of a name for his new pet. Keeping his acceptation sense of direction balanced, he began coming up with names that spun around in his mind. Not this, not that. And definitely not Abdul. Now that was a name the teenager utterly despised. The reason for this was because two years ago he had had a mean teacher he grew to dislike. A name suddenly popped out at him. That was it, Kulade! He could name it Kulade. In his fourth year of school, Patthar had a pen-pal who was apparently from a place called British Columbia. This pen-pal was absolutely obsessed with a flavorful bag called a Kool-Aid. At that time, Patthar thought that British Columbia was perhaps an island between Ireland and the U.K. Now he wasn't so sure. According to his mother, it belonged to a country called Canada. Not just that, but his mother had said that the people there were very strange. When he asked why, Chattan had said that the natives of Canada rode polar bears around and lived in mansions of ice. And apparently they also ate cows for breakfast, lunch, and supper. This was all terrifying news to the young boy and so with a throwing down of the letter he had been sent, he vowed to never write to the girl again. The flashback of thought was abruptly dispelled as a dark-green patch amongst light-brown sand growled at him. That wasn't just a patch; that was a whole rainforest. The colourfully dressed rider finally realized what was happening and where he was. He had somehow gotten off the invisible path he had woven in his mind. He had gotten lost just like before. However, this time it had led him to a large chunk of green, noisy rainforest. That wasn't the problem. The problem was that Patthar might very well become something's meal before the sun fell. Kulade's front hooves touched the mossy ground floor. Her back hooves stayed partially hidden in the dry sand they were all too familiar with. The two froze in terror. There, coming closer and closer from the deepest of the natural city, was a Bengal Tiger. Orange and white stripes decorated its coat and teeth moved as it sneered with its grapefruit-red eyes. The rider slowly edged his hand toward the sultan's scimitar, and soon had the hilt clutched tightly in his dominant hand. There was no way he would be able to escape the majestic creature that saw him as a large, juicy steak. In fact, it was at the moment of this dire situation that Patthar realized that it was either to kill or be killed. Hopping quickly and cautiously off of Kulade's back, he noticed a tension in the Bengal's eyes. It was watching his bladeless weapon and as the sun started glinting off of it's now sudden, shiny, gold form, the Bengal lurched back. Nervous hands dropped the fully elongated weapon into the sand and the tiger sprang into a leap. The victim of the hunt dove for the only thing that would protect him from the Bengal. And the enchanted sword was surprisingly warmer than before as he swung it to touch the tip of the tiger's big, black nose. Its paw was lightly dragging against the boy's stomach. It was ready to deliver the only and final scratch. Instead of killing the innocent passerby, a clash of serenity and calmness overcame him. A fight against the ferocious nature of a wild cat became nothing of the sort. The tiger went back to the rainforest floor and sat down with its paws out. Putting the scimitar back into his trouser belt, the great orange and white started to get up again. Patthar pulled out the scimitar once more and the tiger calmed back to its sitting position. He then took cautious steps toward the tiger and held out his hand while squeezing his eyes closed. Almost expecting his hand to be ripped off, he was surprised when he felt the tiger's fur rub against his palm. When he opened his eyes, he saw that the Bengal was stroking his head against his outreached palm. This act of friendship, sadly, didn't last for long. Before the boy realized what was happening, he heard a hissing from behind and then a flash of orange passed by. There, sitting on the warm ether outside of the rainforest, was the Bengal. It was holding a plump viper between his jaws. He offered it to Boldar's heir, who of course had to decline the offer. Patthar was still full from the party. That and he had never quite liked the taste of viper. Soon after, the large cat disappeared into his very green habitat. And then just like that, Patthar was on Kulade's back again and the journey to the city rolled onward.

A week later, the young traveler made it to the city walls, and he was ready to be done with this entire quest of his. Along the way, he had eaten the rest of the leftovers he had been given by the king and the flask of water was also more than empty. Patthar proceeded through the open gates of the city walls. And to his un-amazement saw that the marketplace was crowded. Navigating through the flood of people, the boy came to a long row of various types of fruit. It was tended to by another Sikh and his turban. He was someone that Patthar's father had been friends with, who might've still been friends with. "Hello, peddler," he addressed the plump fruit seller behind the wooden shelf of coloured edibles.

"How goes it, Patthar? How's your father? How's Boldar?" his fat neck moved around like jello as he spoke.

"He's doing good, Phala Vapari. And so is my mother," the son brought up his other parent. The fruit trader suddenly became deadly quiet.

"Yes…your mother. Um, you have to know that I don't speak of her often. Rarely do, actually," he spoke in a hushed manner.

"It's because she's a *dayan*, right?"

That one statement made the fruit trader act up with frantic energy.

"Shh..., Patthar!" he put a straight finger to his lips. "That's a word that isn't taken well in the whole of India, and the rest of the world. Across the sea and otherwise they call them witches. But if it makes you happy, then yes, she is."

"Does my father know? Why is she one? Is poverty her fault? Did she cause it?"

"Many questions, my young friend. Only one I can answer; he knows. Which means he's looking for you. Leave, and find your father! He mustn't be far from here. I mean I saw him go by here less than two minutes ago. I also saw a group of vicious-looking men. The sort that isn't to be messed with."

"Was the one leading them wearing a patch over his eye?"

"You don't know them, do you?" Phala Vapari worriedly queried.

"I am on a quest, friend of my father. And along the way I met them. They stole from a village that turned out to be a kingdom. These men stole the king's daughter and cow, and I rescued them. I have made enemies that will plague my future."

All of sudden Patthar's eyes enlarged with a fearful thought. He whipped through the pockets of his kurta, coming up empty. Of course, the vest was gonna be empty.

"What is it?" The trader drew closer to the boy.

"Long story, but my father had a map."

"Yes?" His eyes sparkled as they begged for more of what the boy had to say.

"And he sold the map to a merchant. A map that leads to what my quest is entitled to."

"Ah yes, that map!" Phala remarked. "Your father once told me of it, and how he took it from your mother."

"It was my mother's?" Patthar was slowly putting together a giant jigsaw as he went along.

"Chattan was given it a very long time ago, from one of the ancients of our culture. Someone she knew as her father. You think these bandits are looking for the map?"

"Uh huh. But that only means…," the young traveler's sentence was broken.

"That it's very possible that these bandits are actually working with your mother. There's more to this treasure than meets the eye."

"I think you're right. But oh, there are so many questions to this mystery. So many pieces to be fit together."

"Well then, Patthar, I think it's time you go find your father and then get the map before… What's the leader's name?"

"It's Mara. Wait, how did you know they were bandits? I never spoke of bandits."

"I knew him once. He was an old friend, an acquaintance of your father and I. Mara and his men tried to persuade me to join them, mostly because I have a wide book of knowledge up here," Phala pointed to his head. "Knowledge that could aid them with their stealing and pillaging. Though let's not talk about me. I have a feeling he's hiding something he knows about your parents. He's more than what he seems. Anyway, goodbye. I really must be tending to my stand now, and my fruits won't sell themselves."

The fruit merchant went back to selling his wide selection of fruit as the friend he had been talking to went further into the city and around a bend into the end of the marketplace. Rushing ahead, he bumped into a tall, dark-cloaked figure. He looked up to see who it was, and then gasped.

"Hello, old friend," Cetavani sneered. The young quester tried fleeing from his upcoming doom, only to be grabbed by the bandit.

"Let me go, you filthy adult!" the boy yelled at his attacker.

"Fat chance, boy!" The annoyed remark hung in the air as Patthar was dragged toward a curtained opening in a tall building. A mud and sand structure, which in Patthar's eyes, read as 'Bauba's Black Market,' in large not-very neon letters. The curtain was pushed aside and Patthar knew that he had reached his destination. The struggle had been useless and now he calmed down, realizing there was no other way out. And with it, burning tears rolled down his cheeks. Kulade was now in the hands of his mother, Kamadhenu, the goddess of all cows. The worst thing about being in the same room as the bandits was, knowing that it was his fault. He had come to this conclusion when he dreaded the horrible truth and slipped his free hand into the pocket where the note had been bestowed. It was gone.

They had gotten hold of the note. They must have. Where else could it have gone? Patthar thought to himself. The one-eyed man and fellow thieves knew about the map. Before, when the boy had been dragged into Bauba's, Boldar had watched from within the crowd.

He would be waiting for his brother, not to mention his only child. And when the band of individuals left the safety of the Black Market, he would follow in sly pursuit. He moved toward the cow, dragging it as gently as he could by the rope that was tied around its neck. Boldar moved to the outer wall of the shop, and looked into the window. He waited and when the standing was too much for his sore legs, sat down on dusty earth. However, before doing so, he had left the cow partially hidden by a corner of the wall he stood against. He waited ever longer as the sun fell and soon the marketplace grew still and empty. The door opened to the trader's establishment and dark figures stepped out with an unconscious figure held on the shoulder of the giant Bhuka Adami. Boldar abruptly woke up and sleepily got up from his nap. He had just in time avoided the bandit leader's gaze by ducking behind the wall he had been propped against.

"What is it, sir?" The long-bearded Lamba broke the ribbits of frogs.

The leader silently spoke. "Nothing. My eyes deceive me. For a moment, I thought I saw Boldar. But alas, my wretched, and peasant of a brother would never come to confront me. Let us speak no more of it. We shall be silent and go to our camels. To the walls of the desert outside."

As soon as he said this, his band of thieves chortled with laughter. They were just a little drunk. "Shut up, fools; you'll wake a sleeping soul," a light went on in a window as someone with a heavy mane of hair yelled at them to shut up as well. They apologized and were off, leaving segments of conversation floating in the empty air. Boldar took these segments as he leapt away from his hiding spot and pieced them together to form a jigsaw puzzle of what had happened in the enclosed space. The coast was clear and he followed behind at a safe distance, not before retrieving his son's new pet. The thirty-year-old had hidden his camel a couple feet away, tied to a desert oak tree rooted beside a mud hut. Untying the rope that held the camel in place, he got down on a knee and in a whispery voice asked the cow to trust him without being pulled along. In an almost unexpected answer she nodded. This creature was special. There was something about it. It seemed to Patthar's father that the pet acted less and less like a cow as he glanced at it. Untying the makeshift collar around her neck, he hopped onto the back of his camel and rode up to the entrance of the city wall. Over a sand dune, he saw that the band of thieves had started their trek. So, hoping to stay caught up, he sped after them. And following him at a slow trot was the calm cow. Boldar smiled. If the bandits found the treasure, they would be in for a surprise. All things have a catch, that's what he had learned from his dear Chattan. Going back over what he thought happened inside the trading establishment he let his mind guide him through the night. Bauba had sold a map to his guests, and given them dinner for their journey. The man was as greedy and money-hungry as the thieves. Evidently, he had been promised in the end that he would get a share of the khajaana. But, of course, who can trust the words of a thief? Not Boldar, not the son of the greatest thief in all of India.

Time passed as the bandits and their pursuer traveled along a horizon of sand. The sun had pulled itself awake and Boldar was already finished with his morning meal.

It was contained in a cheap, horse-hide pouch. He had shared it with the camel and the newly discovered pursuer, Kulade. But that was an hour ago. And now from what he saw, the band of thieves was gone. They vanished in a cloud of dust that spoiled the calming winds of the desert. Frantically searching for the thieves, Boldar got off from his camel and joined the rough sand below. Next, he assured his companions that he would be back very soon. If he was right, he knew where the bandits were—in the forgotten temple where the map had led, the bhula diya.

Patthar tied the animals to a palm tree with intertwining rope. After, he left. He noticed that five camels were tied to an adjacent palm tree not too far away. A few feet ahead the sand dipped down into a pit that could be walked directly into. He knew where he was. He had been here before. This was where the treasure was hidden. Last time he was here, he had ventured into the temple, and found absolutely nothing. With a descent into the shallow pit, he confronted the vine-covered doors that led into the temple. Boldar had heard talks of how large it had once been. How it had several rooms, a courtyard, and structural advances unimaginable to the human mind. Now, it was one area, the place where worship had once been held. He pulled the opened door even further to his stomach. Then, he stepped into dimness compared to the light of the sun. The exclamation of voices arose and for the first time in two years, Boldar was facing his brother. Boldar spun his head to acknowledge what he saw. Nothing at all had changed. Time wasn't a thing in this dark place. It was non-existent. It kept everything old, never getting older, or younger. Vines broke through sand-coloured stone, and alcoves were indented into the walls. And on either side of the room was a corridor closed in with debris. These were the passages that had once led off into different sections of the temple.

Now that Patthar was awake, he ran to his father with happiness, tears dried from an hour ago. He had always been embarrassed from showing emotion, but today was an exception. Grouped against the far wall were the bandits, where an alcove had long ago been etched into the wall. An alcove where a statue of Buddha had perhaps once stood. The thieves positioned themselves for an attack, and the eye-patched man held an arm out to keep the ones behind him from moving. "Well, well, Brother! Gonna ruin it for me? You gonna spoil the fun of khajaana?" Mara spit and growled at Boldar.

"Thought you were rich, Uncle Mara?" Patthar innocently taunted.

"Why are you doing this? Why are you following an old scrap of paper? I used the map myself, long ago. Stole from my dear Chattan," Boldar followed where his son left off.

"And… you think it was worthless! You never found it, did you, Boldar? You know why you didn't find it?"

The listening bandits by the alcove gasped as Patthar hugged his father with a tight grasp. Boldar patted the boy's head and assured that everything was going to be fine.

"I never did find it, Brother. But that's because there was no khajaana. It's… a stupid map. Now, let Patthar and me go!"

"No, Boldar!" Mara pulled his scimitar from his belt. "You won't leave! In fact, you're gonna learn something. You're gonna learn why you should've never stolen the map from Chattan, your wife."

Boldar pushed Patthar gently away. "Leave my son! If she wants me, if the *dayan* wants me, let her have what she wants. But don't harm my son."

"You hear that? 'Don't harm my son,'" the one-eyed bandit teased. "We don't want him, isn't that right, Chattan?"

From out of a section of the wall, adjacent to the alcove, a figure emerged. Her hair billowed rebelliously behind her dark-grey coat and head-scarf, her *ghoonghat.* And the eyes of a madwoman were beset with a light-blue.

"That's right, Brother-in-law," she smiled menacingly as she came closer to her husband.

“Chattan,” Boldar whispered under his breath with mild shock, “so you were working with him all along?”

“I was. And now you know why I didn’t want you to go with him. It would ruin this scheme of ours. To find khajaana. What belongs to me! And it was all ruined because of our son. He wasn’t the real problem, however; you were!”

“It’s true. I knew what you were a very long time ago, but I learned to forgive and forget! Now, I don’t know if I can. Our son could’ve been in danger because of you. All ’cause I stole your stupid map. I was trying to find a way to stop the poverty. The poverty you caused!” Boldar tried not to sound bitter, but he was.

The uncle interjected. “Wait. What? What is this, Chattan? What have you done?”

“It’s really none of your concern. But I guess you must know. It is after all because of me that you’re no longer rich.”

The bandits gasped and oohed but the ability of making sound effects with their mouth was suddenly quieted with a swish of Chattan’s wrist. The remaining four bandits were turned into statues, and Patthar was left horrified at his mother.

“Aah, Patthar, my son, it’s so good to see you,” she said and became less menacing as she advanced warmly to her son. But no embrace ever occurred. The magical blade was out and pointed straight for Chattan.

“How dare you pull a useless little toy against my mighty powers?” Just like that the enchanted weapon was thrown against the wall of the alcove. Patthar quivered and ran to hide, or so Chattan thought. He was instead retrieving the thrown hilt. There wasn’t any light or sun to be seen. Unless he would move closer to the shut door or used the torch that burned fiercely in its spot on the left-hand side wall.

"What do you mean, Chattan? What did you do?" Mara kept threatening her with his bronze scimitar.

"You see, I once was granted a lamp the colour of the sun. My dying father gave it to me as a present for my twentieth birthday, and I shortly found out that there was a genie inside. At the time I was married to this man, Boldar, and Patthar was soon to come. One day, I took the lamp and by wiping it clean, I met the genie. He gave me three wishes. I wasted the first two on things I now realize are meaningless."

"What were they?" Mara angrily questioned.

She sighed and said, "The first was a happy-ever-after. Which was very stupid to ask for as it doesn't exist. At first, I thought nothing had been changed, but a little while later I could see that the genie had tricked me. Tricked me like he would for the last two wishes."

Boldar made to interrupt her, but he stopped and Chattan continued. "For the second wish, I asked for power. But I didn't mean I wanted to be a witch, a *dayan*. I didn't want that at all," Patthar's mother thought silently before going on. "There I sat at home at the table and I thought that nothing had happened. It didn't work and the jinn had to be fake. So thinking that this would change nothing and the wish-making were all a bit of fun, I wished my last wish. For the last try, I was going to be wise, do something right. Something Boldar would be proud of. He would no longer have to work; we would have all the rupees in India, in Punjab. I wished for never-ending wealth. And I didn't get it. That fiendish genie turned my life into a miserable mess, transformed me into a *dayan* and stole my family's only wealth. That jinn was a sniveling trickster, and he ruined my family! He ruined the only relative that wanted anything to do with us. He made me cold, Brother-in-law, and took away your wealth! Today, Boldar learns that his rich brother isn't so rich after all. Of course, Boldar has known about all of this for a couple of years, haven't you?"

At this, Patthar, Chattan, and Uncle Mara turned to the husband.

Boldar took on a guilty look and said, "Indeed, I was wrong about my own flesh and blood." Then, he looked to the one-eyed bandit with understanding. "And, yes, I found out, rummaging through your diary. You were gone and I'd sensed for a long time that you were keeping something secret. So after you left one day to go to the marketplace, I searched for any shred of what this secret might be. I found it, Chattan, and I was so very horrified. I was angry and still am, so I avenged to get the map back. I only tried from the start to fix your mistake by selling the map for some rupees. I didn't even get much, Chattan; forgive me."

"Oh I forgive you, Boldar. But my cold heart doesn't," she spoke venomously. Then, she changed it all. "So sorry! It's the curse, husband. It's changed me. Get rid of it, please!" Chattan begged.

Everyone silenced their words, only for Patthar to add in a question for the family drama. "Oh why, Father, did you come to look for me?"

"Your mother disappeared and wasn't coming home last morning, so I set off as early as I could from work. And, my Patthar, I feared the worst and knew that your mother's cursed side would be up to no good. I was going to find you, to rescue you from the scheme that would only destroy our house even more. It's not worth it, Chattan! Why would you team up with Mara of all people, to end your poverty? That's not the way! You're only thinking of yourself, and I know I would too," the father pleaded with the mother.

"But oh, it is. You see, with my new powers, I set off to find a cure to what I had done. And unlike you, Husband, I succeeded. I found where the khajaana is. Except, it's locked. It needs a key, Boldar! And I know where the key is!"

"Where?" the bandit leader shouted out with a voice full of greed.

"Don't listen to her! Brother, she's lying; it's a trap, I know it is. There is no treasure; it's only the greed that speaks."

"Be quiet, Husband. This is my job to fix; it was entirely my fault. And guess what, we'll become rich. Rich beyond our wildest dreams. Join us, Boldar!" Chattan invited him with the same menacing grin.

"No, you are no longer my wife. Leave me! The greed, that's the curse the jinn has given you," Boldar said as he held his son close to his side.

"Suits you, Husband. Patthar, give it to me?" Chattan drew out her palm toward the boy.

"What?" he exclaimed.

"You revealed it to me, and I could feel its power. It's the key. The enchanted weapon is the key. It belongs in the alcove. The alcove of innocence. I can sense the hidden wall wanting to be unlocked," she pointed to the farthest alcove on their left-hand side.

"No, I won't give it to you!" Patthar refused.

"Please, Patthar, for Mummy?" she begged innocently.

Her husband shook his head slowly at Patthar. "No!" With that, a frustrated Chattan braced her serpentine digits in a silent dance. A dance that lifted the enchanted scimitar from Patthar's belt, with an invisible pluck of the hand. Patthar's reach wasn't long enough as he tried desperately grabbing it as it floated briskly away. The scimitar was now advancing toward Chattan's outstretched hands. But alas, as soon as its hilt touched her palms, agony showed on her face.

"Aah!" she cried as Patthar caught the falling weapon, and drew it straight toward her heart.

"It's not possible! It's bound to you with some force. It has chosen a master. Therefore, there is only one thing I can do. A thing that will pain me to even think of." With an unnatural speed, she ran directly behind her husband. "If you don't command it to reveal its true purpose, and open the door, I will kill Boldar!"

"But he's your husband! Don't do it! Mother! He loves you! You love him, don't you?"

"It matters no more, Son. I must have the khajaana," Chattan stated shakily.

"Come on, Chattan. You don't; you really don't have to. I know it's the curse that's speaking."

"Silence, puny mortal! You will do as I ask, boy!" she said as she glared at Patthar.

"Please, Mother. I don't want to, but maybe I should. Just maybe it would take away your curse, and free us from poverty," the boy hoped as he found a pre-existing light for a different reason.

"You mean we, Chattan," Mara went back to the talk of khajaana.

"Yes, of course, Brother-in-law, we must have the khajaana. And you will do as I say," she repeated.

"I can't, Mother. I need light."

"Light. Oh, I see! Magic activated by the touch of illumination!" she snapped her fore fingers. Loosening the grip on her husband's neck, she obeyed her son's request. A ball of flame erupted from her other palm and she drew it closer to the hilt held by her son. He brought it even closer to the burning light and within an instant the golden hilt had become a shiny blade.

"All right, I'll help you. But leave my father alone!"

"Come, Brother-in-law, we have something to claim. Lead the way, Patthar!"

Patthar hesitantly led the pair to the far stone alcove. As they gravitated closer to it, a niche only a few inches wide and tall, opened up. It was a key hole that was shaped like the point of Akbar's scimitar, but really like any scimitar for that matter. With a stabbing motion, the keyhole was made complete. Patthar twisted the hilt sharply to the right, spinning it around in a complete circle. Whilst this was happening, the pair of villains behind watched in eager anticipation. A chant had been started by the two, a chant of yes. The key stopped its turning and now a rumbling was evident in the air. The wall shook as the trio stepped back and as Boldar joined them without notice. The wall became still once again. Beyond where the wall had once stood, was another room a tad smaller than the main part of the temple.

Chattan and her accomplice rushed in, forgetting her son and husband. "Finally! Khajaana is mine! It's all mine! And the thought of ridding myself of poverty is exciting my very being."

"You mean, we, Sister-in-law," the uncle corrected.

"Of course, Brother-in-law, of course."

The room was bleak in a sandy-brown, and sadly to the disappointment of Chattan and Mara, there were no giant heaping piles of gold and treasure beyond compare. Instead, in the center of the room was a circular disk of a darker shade of mud. A disk that entrapped an emerald-jeweled mirror in a beam of light. Everyone stepped into the room, one after another, leaving the other four bandits frozen in place like statues.

"Maybe khajaana is still bountiful in here!" Chattan exclaimed as she quietly stared at the mirror. In turn, everyone was so transfixed in their surroundings that Boldar's eyes twinkling and a grin lighting up his defeated face, went unnoticed. Almost.

"What is it, Father?" Patthar prodded his father's ribs with a short finger.

Boldar stammered out an answer, "It might be a second chance to prove that treasure isn't what Chattan thinks. A chance that can both go badly and well at the same time. But I have a feeling it will mostly go well. Or maybe it'll go badly. I don't actually know."

"For you, perhaps, Brother!" the remaining bandit retorted from in front of the group. "But Chattan and I, we're gonna be rich. Unlike you.... you're gonna have the worst of it. Isn't that right, Chattan? There's still khajaana here, isn't there?"

"Yes, that's right. He'll have the worst of it," she spoke as if she was mesmerized by what she saw. "And it's all 'cause I never really loved you, Boldar. Being cursed by that jinn made me realize that. It's because of you I'm not rich. I hate the feeling of being poor. It's... it's awful. And even though that mirror looks pretty useless, I bet the emerald gems on it would make Mara and me very rich."

She then turned to her once-wedded and gave a crooked smile. This wasn't true and Patthar knew it. It was her greed speaking. Chattan impatiently rushed toward the cube with arms outreached after telling her partner in crime to halt his steps.

"How can that be khajaana, Father?"

"I don't know, little Patthar, but I do believe it is treasure of some kind," he whispered in reply.

"But I want to be rich too, Chattan!" the uncle whined.

"Just wait!" she yelled back at him as her hands were inches away from touching the sparkling mirror of emerald.

"Patthar, my father said that I would never find the khajaana on this map. And I never did. I was discouraged when I never found it. But I believe that you have found it. Thanks to Chattan and her accomplice, you've found the way. I, Boldar of Punjab, am proud of you."

Chattan had overheard her name being spoken. "Why thank you, Husband," the *dayan*'s good side started. Then she cackled as her cursed side came back.

"Father, did Dada ever tell you more about what the khajaana was?"

Boldar thoughtfully pondered over the question. Then he said, "Your grandfather did! He said it was a way of changing that which needed to be changed. He also said it was foretold to be made by a powerful jinn that scattered three separate khajanas in India. My father said it had been called 'the mirror of Badalo.'"

"I wonder what he meant by that, changing that which needed to be changed," Boldar said with a shrug.

They were silent again as Chattan stopped, inches away from the mirror of Badalo. "It's ours, Mara, the khajaana is ours!" she reached out to touch the mirror.

"Wait, I beg of you. Can I be first, Mummy? I did lead you here after all," Patthar asked in the nicest possible way he could.

"He did," Boldar agreed.

Chattan thought about it as she turned to face them and said, "Only if I can hold it first."

"Yeah, if only she can hold it first," the uncle repeated.

Patthar stepped up to the mirror of Badalo. "It's you, Patthar, only you can take hold…," But Boldar's words were cut short as the *dayan* snapped his mouth shut.

"Touch the mirror, son of mine," she whispered in serpentine words as she pushed him forward. "Look into the mirror; make us more than rich. And if it may be a magical mirror, we'll be even richer," she cackled again.

"First tell me something, Mother, why did you curse the princess and pet cow of Gannv (gow)?"

"Khajaana! I was trying to find the location of the temple. I became angry when they promised to never tell me," was all she said distractedly.

"It's okay, Father," Patthar assured his father and the worried look he took on. The father simply nodded; he could no longer speak. Then with both hands thrown through the light beam and clamped onto the sides of the mirror, the boy looked through the hazy glass. For a while, nothing happened and the *dayan* showed her disappointment.

"See, it's not magical; it speaks not. Now give me the khajaana; now!" she demanded.

"No, I can hear it… it"s telling me… it's telling me…."

"What! What is it saying, tell me, please, son of mine? I want, khajaana! And I'll take it if you can't tell me what the stupid mirror is saying," she pushed through the boy, ripping him from the jinn mirror. Then, she touched the light beam, and her hand didn't go through; it pressed against it like it was a wall.

"I can't even touch it! Noooo! I want it. It's rightfully mine," she said and looked at Patthar. "What did it say? Tell me."

"It said… it said that the curse makes you a whiny baby. I am the only one that can touch it. I have the scimitar of the sultan. I held it first. Therefore, I opened the door. Besides, you don't want it."

This enraged her and shocked her so much that she let the boy through to look back into the hazy void of the mirror.

The *dayan* then leapt at her one and only son. "If I can't have it, no one can! No one!" rang out her last scream.

"'You can change that which needs to be changed.' What does that mean, mirror?"

The mirror of Badalo spoke in a pitch no one but the chosen could hear. "First, say the word to stop the passing of time. Chattan will pull you away from me, and the curse is at its breaking point. The greed will kill for khajaana."

"What is the word, please? The word? Stop time, you say, how?" As he said this, Chattan and Mara stopped in their tracks, the *dayan*, midway leap, and the uncle by her side with arms reaching out. “Please, what is the word?” the boy asked again, without knowing that he had already said the word.

“You said it, Patthar.”

The boy saw with his eyes that he had stopped time in its footsteps.

“What does it mean, to change what needs to be changed? What are you?”

In a bold voice, the faceless mirror told of what was at hand, “As my name implies. I am change, and the brother of the lamp. You know the lamp of Punjab your mother once had it. But with the words you speak, comes change in your life. I can do anything you say that fixes a part of your world.”

“You mean, I can change the past?”

“Indeed. You can make everything different. Change your mother and father, the poverty you face, rewrite what my brother did.”

“But wouldn’t the erasing of the lamp stop this from ever happening? If I kill the memory of a genie, wouldn’t it ruin my destiny?”

“No, Patthar. It will only stunt the inevitable and change your uncle. He would have never existed and the lie planted in your father’s mind erased.”

“What do you mean uncle? Mirror, please, what does my uncle really have to do with my destiny?”

“I’m the jinn; Uncle Mara is the jinn,” Mara joined the boy. “I faked the time effect on myself. Your parents freed me and then I deleted the memory of faking the effect. I created your uncle, little Patthar. All that exists is Mara, the jinn.”

“But why? Why did you do that? Why are you a trickster?”

"He enjoys it. When we three children of the jinn king were dying, our essences were placed in the three objects of the jinn kingdom. And our malevolent young brother was imprisoned in a lamp, but now he's free."

"How, mirror?"

"He promised Chattan a fourth wish and if she would free him, he would let her redo her wishes."

The jinn took over, "But she didn't know that I couldn't do that. I tricked her into freeing me, and here I am."

"Quickly, Patthar; make a decision! He has the power to destroy me and conquer Punjab, making it his own," the mirror urged him on.

"Don't do it, boy! Let me destroy my brother and I'll take the curse off your mother."

"Never, Mara, I don't think you can. But I think, is it possible, mirror? If I erase him from this point on, will I reverse the wishes and the curse?"

The mirror invisibly nodded, saying, "It's possible, but I am not certain. Do it now before he destroys this place forever!"

The jinn made ready to attack. "Don't listen to him. I must, I must have khajaana! Punjab, my khajaana!"

"He's been cursed as well, hasn't he?"

"My brother, the genie has. Say the final incantation; erase only him. Then you can find the keys of the jinn!"

Patthar's words rose over the words of Badalo. "I… um, command you, mirror, to completely erase the jinn from existence at this point on my road. And with it, may the four wishes and the curse of my family be nonexistent!"

"And...," the mirror prodded.

"Start tomorrow at my mud hut. It's a normal day and Mother and Father are happy. I don't care anymore if we live in poverty or not. As long as what Mara has done is gone. Give Princess Rajakamura a good life to look forward to, and bring the animals and the bandits to where they belong. And most importantly, let me see Kulade's true form. Oh! I almost forgot, only let you and I remember Mara, and his scheme to take over Punjab. Everyone should remember that he's not my uncle. Goodbye, mirror!"

These words were the final things to be heard as Mara was erased, and the family of three was wished away. The secret room in the temple was closed and Akbar's scimitar was back to a hilt in Patthar's possession. Only he and the mirror would remember what happened today. And to the moment when that boy became a man, and then died, he would remember the time he saved Punjab from an evil genie. How he saved his parents and found light through the hard times of living in poverty. How he found truth in all the lies and secrets, and how this would teach him how to deal with such things. His future, after all, would be littered with them. The bandits were brought away to their hidden lair and before Patthar and his parents were wished away, he had a visit from a friend. The Bengal appeared out of nowhere and was now at the very feet of the boy.

"So long, Patthar!" she whispered, "we'll meet again one day, when you're older. And that is a promise I can never break.".

Dazed from everything that had just happened, the boy answered, "Till then. But who are you?"

"I am the one who watches over you. I am your protector, your eternal mother. I am the Bengal."

FIVE YEARS LATER

Twelve year-old Patthar was now no longer that age. He was seventeen, and the words of the Bengal still echoed in his mind. Kulade was now forever his pet, and his parents were now the king and the queen of Punjab. He had asked their permission to go visit a friend, maybe find a bride. For he was old enough to be wedded to someone. And he did hope that a past offer hadn't expired already. The princess who had once been under a spell, whatever had happened to her. Patthar passed by the gate and looked up into the window that had once held a down-looking king. It was the kingdom of Gannv (gow) he had rescued from a spell created by his mother. Now that was something that had never really been fixed by the mirror. The lost kingdom of Gannv (gow) was remembered by no one except him, the young traveler. They didn't even remember the curse that they had had to endure. Patthar looked up at the window and was disappointed by what he saw. The princess was with a tall, black-haired man, and they were surrounded by her people. Patthar had come too late to receive the offer he never took. She was being married as he looked on, and nobody noticed him as he silently stood there, regretting the decision just a little bit.

"She's not the one, Patthar. She never was. The one you're looking for was always with you." He turned to look into the eyes of the old, hunched woman standing next to him.

"I still don't know who you are, Bengal," he said gently.

"No, Patthar, you do. I've always been there with you. I was Kulade after you freed the princess, and then I was the Bengal whom you befriended. I am the one you're looking for. Not a lover but a dear friend that remembers all your adventures."

"My adventures to come? But what, pray tell, are you?" the young traveler asked.

"I am a shape-shifter of nature and not of this world, but you can just call me Bengal."

IIIII2000000000IIIII0IIIII200!:

TRANSLATIONS:

Boldar-'Boulder' in Hindi

Chattan-'Rock' in Hindi

Patthar-'Stone' in Hindi

Kachori-A spicy Indian snack shaped like a round, flattened ball, and made of a flour-based shell containing different kinds of fillings. The most popular filling consists of yellow moong dal, besan flour, pepper, chili powder, cumin seeds, and other spices. Moong dal, is a type of bean cultivated in Eastern and South-Eastern India.

Carabi Itha-'Fat Camel' in Punjabi

Lady Varuna-Water goddess in India

Gannv (pronounced as Gow)-'Village' in Hindi

Bazuraga-'Elder' in Punjabi

Mara–'Bad' in Punjabi

Bauba–'Bob' in Punjabi

Ghoonghat-A head-covering or a headscarf, worn by both single and married women in the Indian subcontinent.

Rajakumari–'Princess' in Hindi

Dukhadai–'Hurrah' in Punjabi

Chole Chickpea Curry-A favorite in North India and consists of chickpeas, onions, tomatoes, garlic, and ginger pastes. It is commonly served with fried Indian leavened bread, like Poori or Bhatura. Poori is fried flatbread, whilst Bhatura is just leavened and fried bread.

Bhukha Adami-'Hungry Man' in Punjabi

Kirpan-A religious dagger, or sword worn by a Sikh at all times. The word Kirpan in its roots means mercy, compassion, honor, and dignity. A Sikh on the other hand is a religion found mostly in Punjab but in all of India and directs itself towards the teachings of Guru Nanak.

Cetavani-Pronounced as Che-Tav-Nee and means 'warning' in Punjabi

Salevara-'Slaver' in Punjabi

Akbar the Great-The king in the 1600s

Lamba-'Longest' in Punjabi

Khanda-A wide, long, and straight Indian sword that's very different from other Indian swords

Gam–'Cow' in Punjabi

Sitar-Is a guitar-like instrument found in the Indian subcontinent, and has nineteen metal strings.

Phala Vapari-Fruit Trader in Punjabi

Khajaana-'Treasure' in Hindi

Bhula Diya-'Forgotten' in Hindi

Jinn-The Arabic word for genie

Badalo-'Change' in Punjabi

GRIM AND HIS WORLD OF MADNESS

ARTIMUS:

Without warning, the reality is gone. I see bright lights as if I had just come out of the darkness. It leaves me overwhelmed. I close my eyes while trying to see, allowing darkness to seep back in. Then with the sound of glass shattering, I'm back to that light. This must be it! This must be reality amongst all the trick's I've seen. And I'm in a cube! The glass to it, it's broken! Yes, it's broken! I can go! Free, I'm free! Wait, why do I sound like this? I'm angry! Oh, it doesn't matter, it doesn't matter! There's a helmet and some wires. There, I got it off. I can get out now! I'm crawling out. And my thoughts, they don't sound angry anymore. I'm starting to remember. Where's my family? I've been taken from them! So has my big bro, Arthur. I get up from off of the dirty floor, to survey a darkened place. It's a large building, and a mahogany staircase leads to a higher level. That's what I see through an open doorway. Steady movement says goodbye to the ugly room. Paint had plastered away to a severe point and the rest of the room was evidence of the dormant state the building should've been in. Now I'm in the entrance where a tall door sits. Glass surrounds it and through it shines what I want to be a happy ending. To be united with my mother, that's what I desire. I must run from this horror that plagues me. But at the same time I'm curious. Where's Arthur? I can't run away, can't escape, without him. So what do I do? I explore. A ten year old in an abandoned place, searching for his thirteen year old brother. Turning my head to the left, I look down a hallway of doors, all open. Then when I arrive at the closest doorway, I take a glance into a room of beds, of course, all empty. Empty of children. And in exchange, on each white linen mattress is a jumble of wires, and a headdress blinking red. I can only guess that my brother escaped. And due to his confrontation with this guy, Grim, he broke the barrier between his reality, and our reality. I see everything. It's horrible. This fractured man saw one solution to his madness. He tried to wipe his guilt away, by giving it to someone else. He tried brainwashing his victims with a false truth. Which reminds me. I gotta find my brother. I have to. So far, each open door, each room, is desolate of life. But before I have the chance to go further down this hallway, there's a creak above me. The mahogany staircase is the way to go. I go back the way I came and start the ascent. I can hear the battling of voices and I think one of them belongs to Arthur. No, that's not true, I *know* one of those is his voice. Slowly but surely I make it to the second set of stairs. Only to be greeted by an alarming noise from outside. Sirens. This can only mean one thing, this is a dream. A dream that my emerald-green sight-seers tell me is real. But what is real? My pace is quickened and I make it to the top layer of what is Grim's house of horror. This is the orphanage that he stayed at from young. It wasn't long ago that I deeply shared that experience. It was my past as well as all the children that had been taken. The darkness is starting to lift. On this final floor is another hallway of doors directly above the last. And a circular window opposite this, looks out at the spring delicacy of the 7th of May. 1953 means nothing to me, or at least it didn't until now. As I look through that small outlet of bright colours, and the representation of a peaceful neighborhood, I notice an obvious detail. A detail so strange that it makes jovial sense. And I'm glad my assumption was right. Arthur and I were not alone. Those vacant beds had been occupied before I had been freed. I was the last to awake. For down below, huddled together in a large swarm, were children. Two police cars and an ambulance waited as the guardians took care of the swarm. The idea of the imprisoned being let out through that one, long door, in a herd, courses out. Time ticks by as I stare out in fascination. s

Soon the swarm spreads out in a rushed chaos. Several varying types of vehicles have arrived and now what I presume are parents, step out. But out of them all, I don't recognize the family-owned Studebaker. Focusing on the reunited down below, I can clearly see the emotion. That, and their arms are reaching out to their lost. What I'm witnessing is families reuniting, something that I must do. The families depart in completion. But by that time, I'm heading in the other direction. A window shuts with a bang somewhere on the top floor, and I attempt to find the source. Once again doors are opened, but this time it doesn't take long before I find what I'm looking for. An open door gives me a full picture of the struggle within. A struggle that sees a light-haired, dark-jacketed man flee from sight.

Out through the open two-frame window, all the way at the far wall. And since there is a fire escape leading from the window sill, he had somewhere to go. Either to the ground below and into the waiting hands of the law, or to the rooftop. Either way, the law would catch him. It always does. My trance falls from Grim's hasty escape and I'm focusing on the only other recipient present. Tears well up in my eyes as I realize who it is. It's Arthur! He's drawing near and for a long moment we stand in each other's arms. We're both wearing expressions of overjoy. And we're unable to stop the never-ending tears that run down our cheeks. These last two months have been a nightmare. But it's going to be different now. The madness that had ensued in two years was in actuality two months. I broke the long hug. "Were you the one that broke the glass of my cube?"

"Yes, I was. Come on, let's go, mom's waiting."

"Did you bring the cops here?" I inquire and hear my accent. We still live in Quebec.

He nods as we descend the staircase. "There was a phone in the back. I'm surprised that he didn't cut the connection. But it makes sense, he wanted this. He wanted to be found."

"Who? Who, Arthur?" I knew it had to be Grim. The question was to be 'Who Was Grim?' A bad man, yes, but one without a face. We're to the door now.

My brother looks at me, "The bad man, Artimus, the bad man. Don't worry about it. After today, he'll go away forever." Arthur pulls the door toward him, releasing a wave of blinding sunlight into my eyes. Blinking it off, I step out into a rainless day. The orphanage leaves us behind and we continue onward. "Remember," Arthur reminisces, "even through hard times, we have to find the light. We have to look for the light in the darkness. And never stop looking till we find it."

"We've been searching for light since the beginning and it's only now that we've actually found it," I add to what my brother has to say. Arthur nods and we leave the orphanage behind. I hope we will never meet or see it again. The part where Arthur and I had been kept in cubes of glass, that still bothers me. "But what about the cubes, why do you think we were the only ones in them?"

"I don't know, Artimus. Don't ask me; all I know is what I saw. He feels as though the kid in him is trapped. Trapped somewhere in a dusty corner of his head." Arthur and I fall into the outstretched arms of our mother. She in turn tells us how much she has missed us, and how hard she had been looking for us. We are reunited at last. With this in mind, Arthur's words stayed true. This was the light I had been searching all along for, and it was finally here. The thing is, as mother was opening the passenger seat of her car, I hear the shocking truth. And I guess my time in the cube warped the details of my identity more than I thought. The truth sends my thoughts in a panic, making me wonder what the connection was. Our lone parent closes the passenger door. I hop over the seat and into the back. And my brother takes the passenger seat as our mother closes the door and walks to the driver's side. It's opened with a pull, and she lowers herself into the Studebaker. The engine awakens with a turn of a key. But instead of us leaving, there is a tap on her glass. It slides into the frame of the door.

"Yes, Officer? Is there anything else I can do for you? Cause I'd like to go home; it's been a long day."

Our mother had young, brown hair and a beautifully plump and flushed face.

"Of course, Mrs. Grim. My name is Michael Jacques. And I would just like to say that you have my partner to thank. She was the one that figured out who the kidnapper was. That and she was the only officer in the precinct who believed we would find them."

The short, messy-haired policeman said his s's with a sounding zee. Then he turns to leave our absent-minded caretaker. Only to come back at the call of his name.

"Make sure you get him," Casey Grim utters with a threatening look.

"We will. We will. And by the way, my partner, her name's Max Radley," he steps aside with a nod of his head. The Studebaker jolts forward and the drive home begins. My name is Artimus Grim and this small detail of my identity confuses me. Who was the man that had taken my brother and me? I knew what he had done, and why. But I don't understand the purpose he had for taking my family's name. There was only one person who it could be. However, it's a theory that would have to wait several more years to have it proven, but I had time.

OFFICER RADLEY:

2 months ago

"When was this?" My thick, French-Canadian accent blurted into the phone's lower-mesh of lines. I was sitting at the desk that had been mine for five years now. It was either gonna stay in my possession or I'd get a new one alongside an upgrade in rank. Due to how everything was looking, the latter could be in my favor. The phone call was to a local tech company that had recently had a break-in. To make my investigation into it worse, the whole police station was in utter panic. Children all over Quebec were going missing. And so far, the only lead we had was an apology letter. That and a suspect no one could find. The reason he couldn't be tracked down was because all we had to go by was a black jacket. One of the parents had apparently seen a mysterious man lurking by their home a couple of weeks ago. A man that was recognized for having a black hood. That was the day the first two had gone. And that was the strangest part of the case. The kidnappings happened with two siblings at a time. The account of the hooded man had days later been added to by a sketch. Unfortunately though, it ended up proving useless when nobody came up in the database scan. According to the worldwide search, the suspect didn't exist. John Doe for no better name; had never been born. This and everything else about the case didn't make sense. There was no identity for the suspect, no motive, and the only evidence to each kidnapping was a letter, and shards of broken glass.

"A week ago, alright. Then, Mr. Larveau, why haven't you alerted the authorities sooner? You only noticed now, okay," my caramel-brown hair bobbed as I tried to solve one of two mysteries.

"I just have one final question and then I'll leave you. Did you see or hear any suspicious people or anybody before the break-in?" I looked up as the commissioner arrived and waited patiently by my desk. The precinct was still buzzing with life and everyone had somewhere to be. "I see, thank you, Mr. Larveau. I'll contact you personally if we find anything."

The phone was put down and the chubby man at the foot of the desk spoke.

"Anything about the million dollar break-in ?" he demanded softly.

"Yes, sir! And I have a hunch that it might be connected with the disappearances."

"How, how might it be connected?" he optimistically faltered.

"Our impossible suspect was at LarTech the week before it happened. And the description even matched with the profile. But that's not it, because he left a name."

"What? What was the name?" an eyebrow shot upward as he became frantic.

"Alfred Mirg."

"Did Larveau say what Mr. Mirg wanted?"

"Yeah. He asked the secretary about their mind analyzer. Of course, Larveau was automatically called and by the time he came down, the man was gone. He seemingly got what he wanted."

"Bon travail, Radley," the commissioner exclaimed. With that, he left for his office, with a look of excitement and a new lead. There was now a name to go with a non-existent face. However, it wouldn't be long before we discovered the name was also non-existent.

Fifteen minutes before the kidnapped were found

I knocked on the commissioner's open door. "Come in," he hollered as I entered the neatly-organized office. "It's been a while since you reported anything. So hopefully, what you have to say changes all that."

"It will, and it has, Commissioner," I said and my smile widened.

"Would you like to sit down?" I shook my head. "Well, then what do you got?"

"I've been thinking about it and I know it seems impossible, but it has to be him. He's the kidnapper! I just know it! The only thing that's bothering me is where he's holding them. That, and why he's doing it."

"Don't tell me who it is," the smile was vanquished from his lips. "I don't care who the vermin is as long as you catch him."

"That's actually good, sir. It's only a hunch," I loudly mumbled. The conversation was paused as a yell was distributed throughout the station.

"Some kid just called, Commissioner! Says that the children are in the old abandoned orphanage on Bleaker's Street."

The commissioner's eyes bulged from their sockets as he heard this and we both looked at each other. Time stopped as I thought about the mystery being solved, and the closure that was being given. Families had been broken, only to now be mended.

"""What are you doing standing there, Officer? Go! And take Jacques and Benoit with you."

I left his office and made one last call at my desk. A call meant for emergencies, now was the time. I was calling an ambulance. Kidnappings usually resulted in a situation where medical attention was needed. The call was quickly finished, and I placed it back on its pedestal. I then summoned my fellow officers to my side, and pushed through the blue double-doors that led to the parking lot. One of them was a short, messy-haired man in his twenties. The other was an older, balder version of the last. Once outside, I split the three of us up into two cars.

"You two take that; I'll take this one," I found myself commanding them. The parking lot of the station was jam packed, like always. And our cars were right by the door, also like always. Benoit and Jacques got into their black and white car with compliancy.

"You can go already. I'll be with you at Bleaker's shortly," I yelled and they both accepted with a, "Yes, madam." Then they were off and I was now standing alone. I was quietly brooding, but that was all let out with a deep breath. I was fantasizing about gaining a promotion by solving the case. Breaking the fantasy off, I was drawn to my four-seater. Once in, I twisted the key in the ignition and buckled my seat belt in. And then, not wanting to stay too far behind the other two, I backed out of the parking lot with ease.

Quebec's Interpol was slowly left behind in its old, stone look of a building. I pressed a button that automatically started the lights and the siren. Smiling to myself, I imagined the panicked faces as the road cleared to let me get to where I needed to be. It was a bit like Moses and the Red Sea, except no staff, and no grumbling crowd. Bleaker street was a five minute drive from where I started. It was also a reminder to the French of Quebec that their history and world had been invaded by the British. The name Bleaker was from a French soldier who had fought in World War 1. The story goes that he betrayed his fellow soldiers for a beautiful woman on the enemy's side. She brainwashed him to go ape-o on the battlefield, and it resulted in a couple of deaths, and his execution. Quebec had named a street after him because it was a reminder that the war had had casualties. It was a reminder that a good soul had been tricked into making a mistake. A mistake that never halted the war. The two-shaded frame of the car went dead and I stepped out by the driver's door. I left it as it was and went to join a chatting Benoit and Jacques by their transport. "Anything yet, Benoit?" I directed my attention to the shortest and hairiest of the pair.

"Nothing, ma'am. But we see ze suspect over zere in ze far window," Benoit pointed to the window next to the fire escape. If the suspect was guilty, then there was a good chance he would try to flee the area. And if he was gonna flee he would most probably use the fire escape.

"He zeems to be zpeaking with zomeone," Jacques spoke with his accent replacing all es' with zees.

"I'm presuming, the child who called and informed us of their location?" Jacques nodded.

"Yes, ma'am! And I propose we keep eyes on the suspect and Arthur Grim."

Benoit and I nodded at Jacques' idea.

"So it was one of ze kidnapped zat called ze precinct? Are we presuming he's part of it, or did he escape to tell us zis information?"

"The latter, Benoit, the latter. He promised us that he would free the others. Besides, I'm expecting Grim to go up the fire escape."

"Grim? You're not zaying what I zink you are, are you?"

"I am, Jacques! But what doesn't make sense, is why Arthur and Artimus? Why kidnap them?"

"He's crooked, ma'am, zat's why!"

"I got that in the beginning, Benoit." The doors to the orphanage swung open and a horde of confused but wildly-relieved children emerged. "Jacques, contact all the parents of the missing. Tell them we've found them. Tell them they're at the old orphanage."

He walked away with the order in mind. Within seconds, everyone that had lost a pair of children was there. They were being returned to their rightful homes. My companions and I were helping as much as we could with the reuniting families, when breaking glass brought my attention to the top floor. The window had been smashed like I knew it would. And a figure in a black hood sped up the steps leading to the rooftop. "Stay here with them. I'm gonna get Grim," I gestured with my right hand. My fellow officers approved with a twitch of their jaws'. Then I raced for the base of the stairs that held tightly to the wall of the building. By the time I had gotten halfway, Grim had already made it to the top of the stairs. The farthest became farther as the lowest made it to the top. We were now both on the rooftop, and I had my hands wrapped around the work-issued handgun. But I hated the idea of using it. This world was and would be forever plagued by the deaths guns had caused. Grim's back was facing me.

"I don't want to shoot you, Grim. I know you know that. Because all I want to do is talk."

"Then put it away, Max Radley," he said in a warm whisper.

"How do you know my name? And why should I trust you? How do I know you won't try to run?"

"It doesn't matter. And you don't know. You can't trust me. But I won't talk if you don't lower the gun and let me go free."

"Not a chance, Mark Grim! That's right. I know who you are as well." A smile was played on my lips. "You're a bad guy, Mark, a bad guy."

"That's very funny, Radley, but you're wrong! You're very wrong! I'm not the bad guy. And if you let me go, I'll tell you why," he sounded American. Which just corroborated my theory due to the Grims' originally coming from America. Or at least the father did.

"Just tell me, what?"

"Oh, alright! I'm not Grim, Radley. You are!"

"No, that's not true. It's not. You're a liar!" Without realizing it, my grip on the kidnapper is loosening. I can't stop it as I'm slowly losing him.

"I'm not, I assure you, Mr. Grim. I saw you kidnap them. You waited for them to go to sleep, all of them. Then you put them into an unconscious slumber using chloroform. This way they wouldn't wake up as you took them." I stayed still as I heard the villain reveal his innocence. I am Grim.

"It's not possible. My name is Max Radley and I'm a police woman for the Quebec Interpol. You're Mark Grim, the father of Arthur and Artimus Grim, and the husband of Casey Grim. But why did you take those innocent lives against their will?"

"Please, Grim. Put away the weapon. I'm not gonna try to run anymore. I want to understand why you're blaming me, Grim. You're the one who did it, after all."

His hands came up to shield himself from the gun. Of course, that was a useless effort. No gun was going to be fired.

"I. Am. Not. You!" I yelled whilst my fingers probed the leather gun sheath by my side. It was now gone from visibility. It had been put away. But it wasn't my will that had done it. At least I don't think so. I think I'm confused about what I believe. I think my mind is being invaded. My real self is being erased by these thoughts that don't belong to me. Am I really Grim? Or am I Max Radley?

"Your resistance to my memories, my thoughts, is stronger than the children's. But I must be honest; you've won. You've defended your mind against my tricks. You're right, I am Grim. And it's true, I'm a bad man," he lifted the hood of the black coat from his lusciously-haired head. It was Alfred Mirg, but he admitted to being Grim. Which could only mean he used plastic surgery to alter himself. This is what I needed him to confess. So I could bridge Mark Grim and the so-called Alfred Mirg together. Even though I knew from the beginning that Mirg wasn't actually the name I needed. It was Grim spelled backwards. And when I checked the list of guardians that had reported their missing, I came across the same last name. Casey Grim. This was the right guy. He even admitted his crime. But that usually meant they had something up their sleeve. "Anyway, I'd better be leaving. And thanks, the gun really helps."

“Don’t you try making a....” It was too late. He was making a run for it. Grim darted behind the hulk of a wooden shed. One that was coated with a layering of chicken wire. This part of the orphanage had once held pigeons. Now it was barren of life besides the chaser and the chased. I was in pursuit of the fleeing kidnapper, and it wasn’t easy. It involved the dodging of obstacles and the holding of a constant speed as I followed Mark Grim to the end of the roof. That, however, didn’t stop him. He had made it to the rooftop belonging to the building behind, with a short jump. I did the same, and landed a dozen inches away. He started running again before I could do anything. Then everything that had happened before in the chase, happened again. Except this time, there was no shed. This time, I had a chance to catch him. And I wouldn’t let him slip away. Another ledge was coming toward us as we weaved through peaks of glass and a few tin chimneys. With another hop, Grim was on the other side. But before he could get any further, I ran and dove off the edge he had left. This was an attempt to make sure this chase didn’t go on any longer. It was a leap toward my goal. And it could go either well, or painfully against the roof. Fortunately I felt success as we both crumpled to the black-tar. I dragged us to our feet. Then in a tightly-clenched hand, I held him by his jacket.

“This doesn’t concern you. I’ll vanish forever from your silly world. Just let me go!”

“Stop the begging, Grim! ’Cause nothing you can say will let you go free. Besides, we still need that talk.”

My hold on Grim is tighter than before. And I’m surprised he’s not trying to escape because he could if he wanted to. “You were brainwashing them with stolen tech. You connected their very minds to a machine that was created by LarTech. But out of it all, you should be ashamed of yourself.”

"Like I said, Radley, I'm a terrible person. I tried to blame them for my life. If my mother hadn't done what she did, I wouldn't be here. However, a part of me still forgives her and I think we should all forgive her. She didn't believe she could raise me on her own. So she did what she could to save a dying planet and left me to fend for myself. She helped with keeping the last city on earth, my earth, alive. My mother, officer, created the city in the valley. But she didn't care about me. Same with my father, he was to blame. For he was the one who caused the ending of the world. Or at least, I think he did. My mother tried to keep everything together while he opposed that. It was a giant fight and I was left to my own survival. Do you know how that feels? To be left alone, and then feel a shred of love before it too gets ripped away." I nodded, he alas didn't believe. "Didn't think so!" Grim shook off the hold I had on him. He paced around, finally content on staying close to me.

"What do you mean, Mark?" I ignored that last bit. "What's the city in the valley? What's your earth? What did your father do to destroy the planet?" The situation was becoming more confusing by what he said. This was all a work of fiction. Mark Grim was truly a madman and an enigma. And like a lot of enigmas, he seemed out of place. I was looking for the truth about why he had done what he had done. But I was also baiting him, trying to help him trust me.

"You just don't get it! You don't know who I am. Because I can see it in your eyes. You still think I'm Mark Grim. But no, I'm nothing like him!"

"Stop lying, Grim. This madness you're trying to inflict has no hold on me. No matter how hard you try, it will always stay your madness. And this world, this city in the valley, it's your world of madness. Grim's world of madness. Because I think I'm getting what you're saying. Your father is Mark Grim, isn't he? And somehow he found another dimension in which you existed instead of your brothers."

He nodded with a smile I found hard to trust. "No one's gonna believe you when you tell them I'm from another dimension."

I matched that with a similar smile. "At least I'll have you in custody." I reached over and whipped out my only pair of handcuffs. Then I clamped one on both mine and Grim's wrist. "At least I'll have proof that you exist, and a name to go with a face."

He pulled on the restraint that had been placed on his right wrist. "Hah! No you don't! You still don't understand who I am! After the asylum, I got a call from my mother who said she wanted to right everything that had gone wrong. I was angry that she only now wanted to be my mother, and that I had gone through a dark life without her. I had accidentally killed someone, getting back for my fiancé's death, and then served my time. Loneliness took me over. I accepted her offer, not knowing what else to do. And then she told me why she wanted to fix what she had done, leaving me in the orphanage when I was young. He had come back. My long-dead father told me that he had found a way to step into other realities. He had grown bored of his world, with its evils, and faults. My father had given up on his side of humanity to see how his family looked like in an alternative to his. He would often switch between both worlds but soon that stopped. He had fallen in love with his new life and vowed to never return to where his real family was. Mark had sent a message to his other family, saying that he was sorry for walking away. He thought he had found a better place. Mark Grim had chosen to stay in the variation of Quebec I had grown to know. It was several years later that I came to the conclusion that I had faked my perfect life to the knowledge of my father. I wanted, due to this conclusion, to really tell of my struggles. I wanted to be able to confide, to talk about life and religion. So I went to my parents' home and I confronted my aged father in his study. Except he wasn't there when I arrived, mother had told me to wait. So I waited until he came back. I waited in secret till he revealed himself. And right then I had the feeling that something was gonna happen. And it did. In a short burst of blue energy, he appeared by his desk. Then he left the private room without suspecting I was there. He had something on his mind and he was constantly checking his watch. Departing from my hiding spot behind a bookshelf, I gravitated toward the desk. My mind was made up and I had a mission that at the time seemed logical. And there was this sneaking hunch that the desk was key. So I maneuvered in a way that I was facing the door in which Mark Grim had gone through. That bookshelf I had hidden behind was diagonally behind the desk. And while I was hiding there in a still form, I noticed something. On the bottom of the desk and at the closest edge to him, was a small device. It was a black, oblong shape that I had never seen in my life. I had only heard stories about what the dimension hopper could do from the man who had experienced it. I bent down an inch and with one of my index fingers I pushed a circular button on it. A funny fizzing sensation erupted all over my body and I felt myself being warped, for no better words. Unconsciousness reigned and the next thing I knew, I was standing on the orphanage." Grim pointed with his non-handcuffed limb.

"Let me guess, your mission was to rid yourself of guilt? And you knew about a machine from your alternate dimension that could do that." I took my chance to speak before he could ramble further.

"It was," he inhaled a breath of fresh air before continuing. "The LarTech in my world designed a machine that could be used to extract memories. But I reversed that and instead I used it to place my memories and thoughts into a mind. All I had to do was find the location for your version of LarTech, and just like that, I had a fully-working model. It was simple. Sadly it's only now that I realize this madness is destroying my understanding of reality. I don't know what's real anymore. And it's getting worse day by day. I am finally getting a taste of my own medicine."

"You know what, Grim? I don't know if I should believe you? But something inside of me is telling me I should. I don't think you're lying, Grim."

"Then if you believe me, that's all you need for proof that I committed the crime."

"Two other things. You didn't try to kidnap your brothers, did you? You just blamed your life on what the two innocent minds represented. They were an uncalled way to finding the light in a world you saw dark and depressing. And what about your father, how did he cause the collapse of earth in your world?"

"I didn't try taking them, I promise. It was a mistake that I should've seen coming. But it caught me off guard." Grim took a break, "as soon as my father entered the dimension with the city, it worsened our situation. Disease crossed over, narrowing the population of the world of Quebec. The city is slowly dying off, and it won't be too long. Quebec became the one city that housed the whole entire world. Anyway, today's the last time you'll ever see me. No one needs to believe any of this. Just let me go, and close the rift we created. We'll leave this place alone!"

"No! You're still coming with me. And just to let you know, I don't have the key," I gestured toward the handcuffs.

He sighed, "Today should've been the last time you ever saw of me. But now I'm afraid you have to come back with me, to the city in the valley. I can't stay here, it could ruin this all."

"I'm not gonna let you vanish like that, monsieur. You are going to come with me and it's high time that we get down from here."

My right and available hand drew closer to the leather encasing my weapon.

"What about what I said? I must go! I'm sorry! I learnt my lesson that you can't make others feel what you've gone through, as close as you've actually felt them. I even gave a message to Artimus's brother. To tell them about their dad. Please, let me go!"

He begged, but I shook my head, "I'm sorry, Grim, whoever you are. You must pay for what you've done here. It doesn't matter if what I've heard is even the truth, you made a mistake to take our children. But why children? Was it because you were a child when you had your hard times?"

He slowly nodded, then let out another sigh. "Before you disappear from your world, I have one more confession to make. I exist in this dimension by another identity. A name you'll recognize very well. My name is Artimus Grim."

Before I could speak another word to describe my astonishment, everything around me was encapsulated by that blue spark. This was the light Grim had spoken about before. And in a way it tied in with the day's revelation. I had finally found my light in the darkness. I had solved the case that had been bothering me from day one. But the question was… would I ever be able to share its results with anybody other than Grim?

Everything was draped in silence. It had been like this as soon as the police officer and the criminal had evaporated into thin air. But like all things, it couldn't last forever. Five minutes rolled by and then with that same abruptness as before, the spark was there.

And then just like that, it vanished for the last time. Because standing there with half a pair of handcuffs on her left wrist, was Max Radley. A whole day had gone by in Grim's dimension and more than anything she wanted to go back to work. There was a lot of explaining to do with the commissioner. But once that was all finished and hopefully she didn't get fired, she had the rest of the day to forget everything that had happened in this case. It was all a madness that never ended. And reality for Max would never be the same again. She had been shown a world where existence balanced on the edge of extinction. To be exact, where the human race balanced on the edge of extinction. She had seen the future from another version of reality. Max Radley had seen the madness. Grim's world of madness. She took the dimension hopper from her pocket and thinking she was doing the right thing, threw it against the tarred-roof. It broke into three chunks, the inner workings hanging out. With that, it felt as if she had done Arthur a justice. She had made absolutely sure that he could never come back. But out of everything she had witnessed in a short amount of time, one thing stuck out as important. There was a lesson in all of this. Each one of us has the power to do evil. But how Radley saw it is that we also have the power to do good.

The End

A=l/0 E=00001 T=20/000002lllll2

Rule: Use the alphabetical and numerical orders side by side. Like above, 1=0/1, 2=01/10, 3=001/110, 4=0001/1110, and 5=00001/01111, until T strikes with a 000002111112/111112000002. Then with U, U=T+0/1